I THINK I MIGHT LOVE YOU

LOVE SISTERS BOOK 1

CHRISTINA C. JONES

WARM HUES CREATIVE

ONE

JACLYN

"*Wrong bitch. Wrong bitch, ayyy. Wrong bitch, yeah you got the wrong bitch.*"

I mouthed along to the music blasting in my ears as I made my way down the hall, with my suitcase rolling behind me. At the door, I twerked a little as I dug through my purse for my overcrowded key ring, sifting through those that went to places that didn't exist anymore, or I refused to step foot in, or where I was no longer welcome, to get to the one I needed. Inside the apartment, I lost the little bit of manners I'd been employing in my three-quarters tipsy state to rap along with Vanity at the top of my voice.

"*Wrong bitch, boy you got the wrong bitch! You ain't slick, boy you did the wrong shit! New niggas, same tricks. Ain't shit, but he want you on his dick! Yeah right, nigga, I'm the wrong chick!*"

I felt that shit.

I felt that shit *deep*.

Stupid ass feelings were to blame for this whole night, actually. I was always *feeling* something.

Ugh.

I let those *feelings* – and my tipsiness – drive me to the freezer, muttering along with *Wrong Bitch* as I checked inside, on the off chance I'd find ice cream that wasn't freezer burned or expired.

Bingo.

I frowned at the "gluten-free, dairy-free, low-sugar, nut-allergy-safe" pint, wondering how the hell that could possibly all work together and why anyone would want it to. I took it from the freezer anyway, then went in search of a spoon. Once I found one, I happily dug in, pleasantly surprised by the taste and texture for it to be a commercial brand.

Ice cream in one hand, spoon in the other, I bopped around the kitchen in semi-darkness as *Wrong Bitch* started up again – I had it on repeat. I hummed along, not a care in the world, until I turned around.

I was *not* alone in the apartment.

The overhead light came on, illuminating the kitchen. My mouth dropped open as I looked into the sleepy, squinted eyes of some light-skinned dude with a fuckboy haircut.

A *naked* light-skinned dude with a fuckboy haircut.

"Who the hell are you?" he asked, hardly audible over the music in my ears.

"You think this shit a game, huh? You think it's funny? Hands up nigga, come up off some money!" Vanity crooned, way too hype for me to *not* be affected by the *fuck-somebody-up* energy she was putting off. That, paired with too much to drink, sprinkled with the natural fear of a naked ass – albeit kinda fine – stranger, fueled what I did next.

I dropped the ice cream and punched him.

Right in the face.

And then, on pure reflex, I drove my knee into his kibbles and bits.

Then, obviously, I ran.

I got my ass away from him, as fast as I could, not realizing until I closed the door behind me I'd run the wrong way.

I was in the bedroom, *further* into the apartment.

"*Come on, Jac!*" I scolded myself, out loud.

This was definitely the most white girl in a scary movie shit I'd ever done.

"*Hey!*" I heard NakedDude bellow, in a deep enough tenor it shook me a little. I locked the door, then dragged the nightstand beside the bed in front of it before I moved into the closet to pull my cell phone from the pocket of the jacket I was still wearing.

I'd dialed the nine and the one before I glanced down, noticing something that made me not press the last number.

Men's shoes.

What the hell were men's shoes doing on the floor of my sister's closet?

That question made me clear the number from my phone as my mind raced to fill in the apparent blank of what in the world was going on. I didn't get much time to think about it though – a sudden pounding on the door made that all but impossible.

"*Wrong bitch, yeah you got the wrong bitch!*"

I snatched the earbuds from my ears, as Dicky McStrangerballs yelled, "*Aye, you got about ten seconds to bring your ass out of there!*"

Yeah.

Mistakes were made.

My fingers moved fast over my screen, dialing Jemma's number as ol' boy pounded on the door. I paced the tiny space

(continued)

of the closet, silently praying that wherever the hell she was, my sister would answer the phone.

"*Bitch pick up the phoooooone,*" I whined, panicking when she hadn't answered after the third ring.

"Wow, Jaclyn," she grumbled into the phone, sounding half-asleep. "Why I gotta be a bitch at six in the morning?"

"*Why is there a stranger in your apartment with his dick out!?*" rushed from my lips as I stepped out of the closet to look around the room. The bed was a mess of sheets, Jemma's perfumes were gone from their usual place on the dresser, and her costume jewelry rack had been replaced by a whole display of hats.

Hats that matched the shoes.

"What?" she asked, losing a little of the sleepiness in her voice. "My apartment... are you talking about Kadan?"

"Who now?"

"My *tenant*, Jac. I sublet my apartment since I'm never there more than a week. *Remember?*"

"Obviously *not*," I countered, cringing as he beat at the door.

"*Aye – I'm calling the cops on your ass in three, two—*"

"Okay!" I shouted at him. "Okay, just gimme a second, damn!"

"You're way too indignant to be on the verge of an assault charge," he called, making me roll my eyes.

He was right, but still.

"Jac, what the hell is going on?!" Jemma squawked before I pulled the phone from my ear, tucking it against my shoulder to move the nightstand from the door. I took my time unlocking and opening it, not at all looking forward to what was waiting on the other side.

Kadan – apparently – was standing there, still naked, looking angry as hell. Like *real* mad.

Big mad.

There was already a purple bruise marbling around his eye, ugly and mottled, messing up an otherwise handsome face. I couldn't help my gaze from drifting down, to his dick – slightly darker than the rest of him, but not purple, at least.

Right?

"What the *fuck* is wrong with you?" he growled, taking a step toward me.

I grinned as I stepped back, holding up my phone to show him Jemma's name on the screen as her voice screeched unintelligibly through the phone's speaker. "One day you're gonna laugh at this," I chuckled, nervously.

He didn't crack a smile. "Not today."

"No," I shook my head. "Nah, not today. Not today at all. We should talk about getting you a discount on next month's rent, huh?"

"We should talk about you getting the hell out of my apartment!" he shot back, making me flinch.

"You ain't gotta use all that bass though, why are you tripping like this?"

"If you don't get your ass—" he muttered, grabbing me by the arm to pull me out of the room, and urge me back toward the kitchen.

"This is *not* necessary," I told him as I snatched away, dropping my phone in the process. I bent to pick it up, ending up with another eyeful of dick as I straightened, but quickly looked away. "It was a mix-up!"

His eyes narrowed, making that bruise look even uglier. "If I'd punched *you*, how would you be reacting right now?"

Ugh.

"Fine. Point taken. But I'm sorry, okay? Seriously. I'm Jemma's sister, and I have a key. I didn't know—"

"Yeah, yeah, get your shit and go."

He pointed toward the cactus-colored, rolling carryon parked next to the kitchen counter. When I didn't move – out of sheer stubbornness – he moved to get it for me, prompting me into action before he tossed it out a window or something.

"It's been *very* unpleasant to meet you," I grumbled as I grabbed the handle of my bag. "And I *won't* be looking into that rent discount."

"Look into not letting the door hit you on the way out, how about that?"

My mouth dropped. *"Rude!"*

The look he gave me after that was a clear indication he'd reached the end of his inexplicable patience with me. I rushed to the door with him right on my heels, and once I was on the other side, I turned to say one last thing.

I was met with a slammed door in my face.

"Asshole!" I shouted at the closed door.

"Ya mama!" he yelled back, making my eyes spring wide. The only thing that kept me from knocking on the door again was the ringing of my cell, which a quick glance told me was Jemma calling back.

"What?!" I answered, with unfounded attitude as I scowled at her door one more time before I started down the hall.

"Girl, *simmer*," Jemma insisted, still only sounding half-awake. "What the hell is going on? What the hell was all that commotion, and why is my tenant calling me?"

"To tattle," I whined, pushing a handful of locs over my

shoulder. "I may or may not have punched him in the eye. And kneed him in the nuts."

Damn.

No wonder he was mad.

"Jac, what the *hell*?"

"*You* told me I could use that key whenever I needed to! I didn't think I needed to call you, because I knew *you* weren't there. You're in Liberia or something."

"Ethiopia," she corrected. "And I definitely mentioned renting my place out."

"Probably to Joia – not to me."

"*Jac*."

"*Jem*," I shot back, not appreciating her scolding tone. "Whatever happened, I didn't know anybody was there, and I needed a place to crash for the night."

Ugh.

I climbed onto the elevator with an awful taste in my mouth from too much to drink, and a throbbing head from too much drama.

"A place to crash why?" she asked. "You have a whole ass apartment with your boyfriend."

A deep sigh left my throat as I closed my eyes, and the elevator started moving. "*Ex*-boyfriend."

"*What?*" she exclaimed, exactly the reaction I had not been looking forward to.

I shrugged. "I dumped his ass, after he left me for his *wife*."

"*Excuse me?*"

"Nope. You heard right," I assured, squinting against the bright light in the lobby. "I thought his ass was traveling for work – turns out I'm his second family."

Jemma sucked her teeth. "Jac, stop lying."

"Hand to God, big sister," I declared, looking up one side of the street, then the other, trying to get my bearings. "She knew about me, sort of. Didn't know we were living together until she got his credit card statements, or something, hell, I don't know. She was fine knowing he was fucking someone else, but I guess a full-blown relationship was too much. Her ass *called me.*"

Jemma let out a long sigh before she spoke again. "I'm sorry that happened to you boo."

I shrugged. "Oh well. One fuckboy don't stop *this* show. I'm gonna see if I can impose on Joia long enough to sleep and get cleaned up. And then go apartment hunting, I guess."

"I'm sure she won't mind," Jem yawned, and I had to press my lips together to keep from mimicking it. "You have a key to her place too, don't you?"

"Yes, but I think I've learned my lesson about not calling first. I'd rather not run into another naked stranger."

"Wait, *naked*?" Jemma gasped. "You didn't say anything about – *ooooh*, you *did!* You said his dick was out, didn't you?"

"I did."

"So...?"

I frowned. "So, *what?*"

"So how was it, duh! Long, short, skinny, thick... details, bitch!"

"I was too busy trying not to get murdered to be concerned about his dick!"

"Jac..."

"Okay so it was a good six, but it was soft, so we could be dealing with a grower – a passing grade either way, especially when accounting for girth, which appeared to be substantial. Not too much hair, not too little either. Slightly darker than his body. Even coloring. Not ashy. No odor."

"That's important!" Jemma chimed.

"*Very*," I agreed. "Overall, a strong showing at this year's, *I Wasn't Even Trying To See It, But There It Was,* Dicklympics."

Jemma broke down laughing, but quickly stopped. "Oop. That's him calling me again now."

I rolled my eyes. "Don't give him a rent discount."

"Didn't you punch him in the eye and knee his balls? Girl I love you, but I can't be getting sued fooling with you!"

"He was *mean!*"

"You assaulted him!" Jemma shot back, dramatic if you asked me, but I guess she had a point.

"*Fiiiine,*" I groaned. "I'll cover whatever you have to give him."

"Okay now tell me something I *didn't* know."

"Get off the phone and talk to your tenant."

"Bye!"

I hung up the phone and let out a sigh before I immediately moved to dial our middle sister, Joia. I gave her a bare-bones explanation of what I needed, getting approval to spend the night at her place.

I blew out a sigh, and switched apps to order a ride.

I hadn't completed the transaction yet when a police car pulled up to the curb, and two officers jumped out. My eyes went wide as they came straight to me, hands on their weapons.

"Are you Jaclyn Love?" one asked, shifting my wide-eyed gaze to a frown.

"Who's asking?"

The who *hadn't* asked smirked. "Ms. Love, we need you to come with us – we got a report of vandalism, threats of violence, and destruction of property from a Victor Isaacs?"

"Oh no, you've got the wrong person," I said immediately, shaking my head. "Anyway, how did you find me?"

"According to Mr. Isaacs, you screamed …" the officer pulled a tablet from somewhere, holding it up to see the screen. "I quote – I'd rather be a hobo bitch than look at your bitch ass face one more minute. You are hiding a child! Fuck you. I'm going to my sister's, but I'll be back for your ass, bitch."

My head tipped to the side. "Who said that? *I* said that?!"

"Yes ma'am, you did. He gave us the address."

"Okay, fine. I said that, but I was mad. Everybody says things when they're mad. You're here to arrest me about that?"

The officer without the tablet shook his head. "No ma'am. We're here to arrest you for the brick through the window of his Mercedes, the slashed tires, and the spray paint."

"Well that's ridiculous, I didn't—"

"So this isn't you, earlier tonight?" the officer with the tablet asked, holding it up to show me a video playing on the screen.

Surveillance, from the parking garage.

With audio.

The tires were already flat, and the brick was already through the window. But there I was, locs swinging, rapping *Wrong Bitch* at the top of my lungs while I spray-painted those same words on the hood of Victor's precious black Mercedes.

My other hand held a bottle of vodka.

I closed my eyes, stashing my cell phone in my pocket before I held my hands up in front of me, hoping at least for a peaceful ride to the station.

They got the right bitch today.

TWO

JACLYN

FOUR HUNDRED HOURS OF COMMUNITY SERVICE.

Four *hundred* hours of community service.

That was the price to be paid for my drunken shenanigans with Victor's car.

Carrie Underwood and Jazmine Sullivan had me out here bad.

While I couldn't say damaging his property had been worth it – I still felt like shit afterward, and now I was paying for it – I definitely found myself grateful for *this* punishment, cause it could've been worse.

It could've been a *lot* worse.

As harsh as it sounded, four hundred hours of community service sounded a helluva lot better than jail time, and certainly worked better for my life.

Something I should've considered before my anger and alcohol consumption got the best of me. I was already scarcely holding my shit together, between being a full-time student *and* running *The Dreamery* – the tiny ice cream franchise that paid my bills, at only twenty-four years old. I didn't have time for four hundred hours of community service.

But I was going to have to find it.

It hadn't taken much to find a new place of my own. Blakewood was built specifically around the local university, so there was always space somewhere. According to the history, the school was founded by Blackwood natives, looking to escape the big city. Thousands of miles West, they found the perfect space – naming it *Blake*wood, a portmanteau of the largest investor's name and the city they'd left, but still wanted to honor. Of course it started small, no accreditation, but a hundred years later, Blakewood was a force.

It was also home.

My new place was small, but it was *mine*, and I was in no big hurry for a change in status – not this time. I was tired of *trying* to get my life together, and ready to just *do it*. No relationship drama distracting me, no man taking up my limited time – just me, focusing on *me*.

The apartment had come furnished – something I'd gladly paid a premium for, to avoid the hassle and immediate expense of having to buy everything myself. All I'd had to bring were my personal belongings, plugging them into ready-made comfort, which was relieving.

I settled onto the couch, laptop in hand, to do a little research. The judge had given me a specific list of places where I could fulfill my service hours, and I was *not* trying to end up raking leaves at the park, or picking up trash off the side of the road.

I'd already done both of those.

A strange sound outside the window behind me pulled my attention away from the laptop. It had been pouring rain for hours while I did my homework, so I hadn't thought much of anything coming from out there, knowing how storms amplified everything. But now that my attention wasn't quite as focused, I heard it again.

A mournful, plaintive whine... the kind that came from a cat.

Instantly, my nose wrinkled.

There was only room for *one* pussy around here.

I rummaged through the kitchen drawers to find a flashlight, then went back to the window. The building had fire escapes, which gave me protection from the rain as I opened the window and peered out, looking around for what I assumed would be a neighbor's cat, so I could shoo it away.

What if it runs in through the open window though?

That thought made me narrow my eyes, suspicious of MysteryCat as the beam of my flashlight landed on fur. It was tucked into a corner nearly out of sight, and I realized my concern was unfounded. That cat wasn't "running" anywhere, not with that big ass patch of missing fur, and bleeding gash.

"*Dammit,*" I muttered, pushing out a sigh.

I didn't have time for this.

Tucking my head back inside the window, I closed and locked it, and put the flashlight away. I moved back to the couch, where my cell phone was, to look up my options for having dinner brought to me so I could eat while I decided which punishment I would endure. Did I have food in my fridge?

Yes.

Did I *want* that?

No.

But what about the cat, Jaclyn?

... what about it?

I was nobody's animal person, and hadn't told her ass to climb up to *my* window.

Homegirl had to figure her own shit out.

With that said, those sad ass *meows* seemed to grow louder, and louder, and *louder,* the same weird shit, over and over.

"Girl will you shut up?!" I yelled at the window, then turned back to my phone, scrolling through my list of options.

MysteryCat did not, in fact, shut up, which prompted me to let out yet another sigh.

Fine.

Maybe I could give her something to eat, at least. She couldn't keep up all that hollering with food in her mouth.

Annoyed as hell about it, I trudged to the kitchen, looking through the cabinets until I found a bowl. Opening the fridge, I glanced at the few items I'd grabbed at the grocery store, and determined the pre-cooked chicken was the best option from my meager groceries.

I put a few pieces in the bowl – then stopped to check the internet to make sure cats could even eat chicken – then went back to the window, stepping out onto the fire escape this time. I slid the bowl to her, close enough she wouldn't have to move too much to get to it. That heifer took one sniff, looked at me, then put her head down without even touching it.

I sucked my teeth. "Okay, I *know* your ass isn't being picky?" I pushed the bowl closer, prompting her to lift her head for another long *"bitch, can't you tell I don't want this??"* stare.

"Well, *fine!* Ungrateful ass," I snapped, leaving the bowl as I moved to go back inside.

Then she wanted to start that *"meow"* -ing again, making it clear she had no plans of letting me have any peace tonight.

"What more do you want from me?" I whined, pouting as I

climbed back into my apartment. I picked up my phone for a new search on my internet browser.

Blakewood veterinarians

I frowned at all the cutesy ass names that came up first, scrolling right past all of those to get to *Blakewood Animal Clinic,* which was the only one still open anyway. A quick glance at their website showed enough melanin from the various images on the home screen that I was comfortable giving them my business.

I went back to the kitchen, searching under the sink for a pair of rubber gloves.

"*Yass,*" I mumbled to myself, doing a shimmy when I discovered a pair of rubber dish gloves under there, which I opened and put on before I straightened again. Looking around, I regretted asking the movers to take all the extra boxes with them – even *one* would be helpful now. Pursing my lips, I turned to the cabinets again, doing another triumphant dance when I spotted a big plastic mixing bowl – part of the "furnished" apartment – that looked cheap enough I wouldn't mind replacing it.

Do I need a spatula too?

Maybe not.

Probably not.

After testing the thickness of the gloves, in case *MysteryCat* decided to try to scratch or bite, I took the bowl back out onto the fire escape with me, and did my best to gently transfer her into the bowl. Once she was in there, she seemed so *small*. Much smaller than I'd expected. Feeling bad for the abundance of skin and fur – and lack of thickness – I saw, I put the chicken in the bowl with her after a few seconds of thought.

Maybe she'd get hungry on the way.

I brought the bowl inside, leaving it on my counter while I put on shoes and a jacket, and found an umbrella. The clinic was only a block away, so I didn't bother using my rideshare app, choosing instead to walk.

Blakewood Animal Clinic was by no means a fancy establishment, if the outside was any indication. The sign was broken – but clean – and the only outside décor was hand-drawn paws and claws and other animal-related signs and symbols, done in dry-erase marker on the inside of the windows.

The waiting room was empty when I stepped in, but the chime over the door must have alerted someone to my presence. A handsome Asian man with tatted arms came from the back with a puppy wearing a cone around its' neck in his arms, followed closely by a black woman with a clipboard and a smile.

"Can we help you?" she asked, her expression changing as her eyes landed on the bowl in my hands.

"Uh, yeah," I told her, holding it out. "I found this cat on my fire escape. I think it… I don't know. Got attacked by a dog or something. Maybe."

"Aww, poor thing," the man said, and ol' girl about swooned out of her scrubs grinning at him as he stepped forward to peek into the bowl. "Char will get you taken care of," he told me, then turned to her. "I'm going to get this guy tucked away for the night, and I'll let Dr. Davenport know we have a new patient."

"Thanks Kenzo," she gushed, watching him as he walked away.

I didn't blame her either.

He had ass in those scrubs.

Once he was through that door, I cleared my throat, pulling her attention back to me.

"*Sorry*," she breathed, her light brown skin flushing as she hurried to the reception desk.

"Oh girl, you're good. I get it. He fine. You hittin' that?" I asked, knowing it was bold as hell, but I was curious. My question only made her blush harder as she shook her head.

"No. I *wish*," she whispered, damn near to herself, after glancing over her shoulder to make sure he wasn't there. "Um, okay, let's get some information down about your injured pet."

"Oh no, she's not my pet," I corrected, wanting to make that shit *clear*. "I was just minding my business, trying to work, and this thing started making all kinda noise on my fire escape. All I want is quiet."

The girl – *Char* – looked horrified, eyes wide, lips parted. "Oh. Um, okay. So I'm guessing there's no name?"

"I'm not even trying to take this thing home," I admitted. "I thought I saw you guys had animal shelter affiliation or something?"

"We *do*, but—"

"Okay so yeah, I wanna do that. Sew her up or whatever, and then take her off my hands. I don't have time to play nurse."

"Char?" a voice – a *different* voice – called, from around the corner where Kenzo had disappeared. It seemed to be getting closer – and more familiar – as he continued speaking. "Ken said we had a pa—ah, *hell*."

Ah hell, indeed.

If I was "Dr. Davenport", I wouldn't want to see me either.

He stopped on the other side of the desk, looking better than he had any business looking in bright blue scrubs. There was a surgical mask hooked over his ears, but pushed down under his chin in a way that made it cup his beard, something that had, undoubtedly, made more than one child giggle today.

Hell.

It had *me* feeling giggly too, or at least it would've, if it wasn't for the faint remnants of purple mottled bruises surrounding his eye, from where I'd punched him two weeks ago.

"What is this?" he asked. "You back to finish the job?"

I smirked. "That's funny, but I can assure you – I had *no* idea you'd be here. I don't even know you."

"Really?" he asked, eyebrow lifted. "I'd say you're quite familiar."

Something about those words was like flipping on a magnetized field. Instantly, my gaze dropped to his groin area, and... sweatpants are cool and all, but have you ever seen a dick print in scrubs? A thinner, stiffer fabric meant a more pronounced... contour.

"I don't recall," I lied right to his face, pressing my lips together and crossing my arms, daring him to offer a comeback in front of his coworker, who was looking back and forth between us.

"*Ohh!*" Char exclaimed, snapping her fingers. "Is this the homeless woman you found in your apartment?! The one who punched you in the eye?!'

I gasped. "*I have a home!*"

"Could've fooled me," Kadan replied, in the smug tone of a man who *knew* he'd scored a point in what was now, apparently, a back and forth.

My mouth opened, intent on offering a witty response, but all I could stammer was, "I was having a bad night, for your information." I hiked my nose up in the air, gesturing toward the cat, who was currently looking at all of us like we were crazy.

"Now if you're done – here is this animal. Heal it, or whatever. You can send the bill to my *home*."

Kadan frowned. "Why is it in a mixing bowl with... is that *chicken?* What is wrong with you, woman?"

"*I thought she might get hungry!*"

"Or *you* were hungry."

My eyes narrowed. "I don't eat pussy, I am *strictly* dickly, excuse you."

"That puts a lot in perspective."

"Nigga can you just fix the goddamn cat?! Please?!" I snapped, propping a hand on my hip. "I have *other* shit to do."

Kadan – and Char, for that matter – frowned. "I'm sure your suffering pet has a name you could call her by, instead of *goddamn cat.*"

"She is *not* my pet, first of all, and I don't even know if she is actually a she. It showed up on my fire escape, crying like Whitley Gilbert. *Dwayyyne. Dwayyyyne.* That's what the shit sounds like!"

With a deep sigh, Kadan lifted the bowl in one arm, using his free hand to run over the cat's head, soothing her. "What do you *think* happened?"

I shrugged. "I have no idea, but my best guess is she got attacked by a dog or something. I don't know."

"Okay. I'm going to take her in the back and get her checked out. Wait here."

"Okay but like I wasn't even trying to bring her back with me!" I yelled at his back, as he completely ignored me. I growled my frustration, then turned back to where Char was waiting, thinly-veiled amusement on her face.

"Will that be cash, check or credit today?"

THREE

KADAN

So... I couldn't even front on Jaclyn.

Ol' girl was fine.

Like *extra* fine.

Risk it all fine.

Problem was, she was a lunatic, evidenced by her busting me in my shit in my own house, getting arrested on the street after – which I saw through the window after I looked out to make sure Jemma's assurance she'd left the building wasn't a lie – and now, her ass bringing an injured cat in a bowl of chicken in here.

But Kadan, ain't that the type of shenanigans you're a sucker for? <- the question I could count on from anybody who knew me, especially if they laid eyes on Jaclyn. The locs, the deep brown skin, the lips, the *thighs*, goddamn. Her whole erratic thicksnack situation was *exactly* my type.

Like... *exactly* my type.

Exactly.

It was also the type I was supposed to be off of, because I was getting too old for that volatile shit. Sure, plenty of people were happy to live with the stress of great sex and high drama well past their early thirties – my father was one. But one of the last things he said to me was, "High-quality pussy ain't never done nothing to nobody. Look at me! I keep myself a steady supply of women that might stab your ass. Just don't do nothing to get stabbed and don't worry about it. Unpredictable pussy ain't gone kill you, don't be scared now!"

He died of a heart attack two days later, at sixty-three.

Mid-coitus.

So.

Yeah.

Was *not* trying to go out like that.

So I sewed up the cat – the injured one, that Jac brought in.

I agreed with her assessment that she – the cat – had likely had a bad run-in with a dog. Luckily, it wasn't too serious of an injury – I sedated her, washed the wound, and stitched her closed, then put together the cocktail of painkillers and antibiotics Jaclyn would need to make sure the cat stayed comfortable and uninfected.

If she was even still here.

I'd caught her comments about not planning to keep the cat, but had ignored them, in hopes she'd have a change of heart. She could've not bothered with the cat at all, but the fact she'd taken the time to get it here to the clinic before we closed... I had a feeling we could change her mind.

I put the cat in a *proper* carrier, and grabbed food from our stock as well, carrying it all up to the waiting room. Char and Kenzo were hanging close as hell in the tiny corner of the front desk that was hidden from customers by the wall – just talking, as far as I could tell, but they parted at the sound of my footsteps.

Like they were fooling anybody.

"She still here?" I asked, holding up the cat carrier in one hand, and the bag of supplies in the other.

Flustered, Char nodded. "Uh, yeah, but she fell asleep like twenty minutes ago."

"Probably exhausted from a long day of giving people hell," I muttered as I rounded the corner, stepping out into the waiting room.

Just as Char said, Jaclyn was fast asleep, her legs stretched across several chairs and her head resting against the wall. With her eyes closed, lips slightly parted, locs falling over her face, glasses cocked crookedly against her nose, she almost looked *sweet*.

Good thing I knew better.

"*Ms. Love*," I called, tapping the chair she was sitting in with my foot to get her attention. Her eyes popped open with a sharp intake of breath, and instinct warned me to get back – *right* on time.

Still – mostly – asleep, Jaclyn popped up from her chair swinging, prompting a collective chorus of "*Whoa!*" from me, Kenzo, and Char.

The sound of our voices seemed to pull Jaclyn further into reality, but just a little. Her face pulled into a squint as she looked around, confused, then moved to push her glasses into the right place.

"You can put those fists away, McNabb," I teased her, earning an even deeper scowl than she was already wearing. "You've got other things to occupy your hands." I held the carrier and the bag of supplies out to her, and she reluctantly accepted.

"How am I supposed to defend myself, if both hands are full?"

"Just swing what's in your hand..."

"*Oh.*" She glanced thoughtfully down at the cat carrier. "I guess this thing *is* pretty heavy duty. I could knock a motherfucker out."

"I was talking about what you had in the *other* hand, but go off I guess," I told her, less confident about the safety of the cat if her first thought was to swing *that* at somebody.

"So what's wrong with her? What is all this stuff in the bag, and how much *more* is it costing me?"

I shook my head. "Costs you nothing. You pay for the visit, and we provide everything else, unless your pet needed major care. This girl got lucky – and she is, indeed, female."

"Good for her – still not my pet," Jaclyn corrected me. "What all am I supposed to be doing for her?"

"Just give her the meds, don't let her jump around, and don't let her chew at her stitches. I put a collar on her, which should discourage the chewing, but still keep an eye out. And make sure the incision doesn't start looking bad – leaking, swelling, any of that."

When I finished that short spiel, Jaclyn was looking at me with wide eyes, trying to absorb everything I'd said. But then, she shook her head.

"Listen – I run a business, and I'm trying to finish a degree, and I have a new responsibility that popped up, that's going to require even more of me. I don't have time to take care of this cat."

I shrugged. "Everybody's busy Jaclyn. I promise you, it sounds like more than it is – it'll only take a few minutes out of your day."

"*Minutes I don't have,*" she muttered under her breath, rolling her eyes before she brought her attention back to my face. "Fine. I'll give it a shot because I feel bad for Miss Thing, but do *not* be surprised if I come back in a few days to drop this carrier at the desk and walk right on outta here."

"I think you and your new pet are going to get along fine Ms. Love," I encouraged. "I even stuck a litter box and stuff in that bag for you, to put you on a path to success."

She narrowed her eyes. "I want you to know I recognize a setup when I see it. I wanna remind you, I know where you live."

"Ain't no set up, woman," I shot back, alarmed. "I'm trying to help you."

"If you were trying to help *me,* I wouldn't be taking this cat home, bruh." She pushed out a sigh. "We done here?"

"We are."

"Good."

With that, she turned and walked out the clinic door, leaving me quite confident if one of her hands had been free, I would've gotten flipped off. Char and Kenzo had been hiding out once Jaclyn woke up swinging, but now they both stepped into the waiting room to join me.

"I like her," Char hummed, turning to grin at me and Kenzo.

"*You?*" I asked, surprised. "Sweet, pleasant Char, like *her?*"

Crossing her arms, she nodded. "Yep. Because I am over thirty, and tired of my go-to adjectives being 'sweet and pleasant' like I'm a cupcake."

"But you *are* like a cupcake," Kenzo told her, words that inexplicably made her blush, considering she'd *just* presented the same descriptor as a negative. "Everybody likes cupcakes."

Those words took her smile down a few notches.

"Not everybody," she countered, a sudden hint of sadness coloring her tone. "Anyway, I'm going to head out. It's been a *long* day."

I cringed. "Yeah, sorry about that Char. I've tried to tell the city we need *more* help here."

Kenzo chuckled, clapping me on the shoulder. "They exhausted the budget bringing *you* in, man. Can't afford more help unless they change the payment structure, and you know that's not happening."

Definitely wasn't happening.

"You were a necessary addition though," Char chimed in, ready to make sure there were no bruised feelings. "The caseload was so heavy before you came we were having to turn away everything except the most serious cases, and Kenzo was so busy I don't think he even knew my name."

Ken frowned. "I knew your name."

"But you were calling me *desk girl,*" she countered.

"Not like, *desk girl,*" he argued. "Like, *Desk Girl!* Like a superhero, cause you were keeping everything in order, saving the day..."

Char's eyebrows went up. "*Oh.* Oh. I never thought about it like that. But I'm a *woman.* Not a girl. Goodnight guys," she said, pushing through the door that led to the back, and disappearing.

As soon as she was out of earshot, I put on my stern face and turned to Kenzo. "When are you going to stop playing and ask her out?"

He smirked. "When am I supposed to do that? You always have her working the desk."

"Oh *I* do," I laughed. "You know we're rarely here past nine pm. Plenty of time for a date."

Ken shook his head. "Good girl like that expects dinner at seven, home by ten, panties intact. *Not* my type of date."

"So you're going to keep flirting instead of doing anything about it because you think she's not gonna let you hit on the first date?" I asked.

"Nope – I'm going to keep flirting and not doing anything about it because I know damn well she's not in the market for what I can offer. A girl like that wants the house, the kids, the *ring*."

"She already told you about that *girl* shit," I laughed. "You keep saying what *a girl like that* wants, what she expects, but have you bothered to ask the *woman*, Char, what it is she wants?"

"I *know* women," Ken assured me. "Trust me, I've got this."

I chuckled. "Aiight man – you think you got it, so I'ma let you have it... as long as you're not playing with her emotions."

"Fair enough," Kenzo agreed, returning the gesture when I held my fist out to him.

Twenty minutes later, we'd closed up for the night and all gone our separate ways, with me heading back to the apartment I was subletting from Jaclyn's sister, Jemma. I'd been grateful for the place – it was nice as hell, and a decent distance from where the college kids seemed to congregate, and mostly outside of their price range, so I didn't find myself living among a bunch of young adults.

For one, I didn't have the patience, and secondly, I couldn't handle the noise, or the big crowds of people that seemed to be a native part of living too near a college. I'd spent enough time in my 20s around strange people and excess noise – and not the innocent kind I was avoiding now. As an army veteran, I'd seen *combat*, and I wasn't trying to be near anything that even vaguely reminded me of that.

Hell, when I discharged, I didn't even want to take my skills as a trained medic into the real world with me – at least, not to work on people. Instead, I took that passion with me to veterinary school, then came back to the town where I'd grown up to put it all to use.

Fuck those college kids though.

It hadn't been surprising at all to learn Jaclyn was one of them. She didn't look particularly young –was a grown ass woman – but she rankled my nerves in the same way. She *was* young enough that the business owner thing threw me, but for all I knew, her "business" could be selling pictures of her feet on the internet or something.

I could look into it, if I felt inclined.

And honestly speaking, part of me did feel inclined, but I had zero intention of listening to *that* shit, because I knew how it would go. I'd look her up to find out more, and knowing more would make me want to know *even more*, and before I knew it, I'd be balls deep in Jaclyn Love with no idea how to pull myself out, and I didn't get the impression she was the kind of woman who'd help.

Not that she'd be stuck on me.

In fact, I highly doubted she would, which made the whole idea even more attractive – and made it even more important to stay away from. When I was younger, I'd followed my father's advice religiously – he was the *man*, and I looked up to him. He was a proud proponent of hoeing, so that's what I did, and I wouldn't even try to pretend I hadn't enjoyed it. The sex, the liquor, the drama... the shit had been fun.

Until that lifestyle showed what it cost.

Last year, when I lost him, I'd vowed right there at the funeral – while the woman who gave him the heart attack physically fought the woman he was "officially" dating – that I wasn't going to do it anymore. While the family was busy breaking them up, I was busy going over a game plan in my mind – how to *not* be like my old man.

In many ways, my father was a great person – he'd just set the worst possible example of a healthy love life, even in his relationship with my mother. There were plenty of ways to honor him, but following in those particular footsteps wasn't it.

I was *not* about to end up in an early grave like him.

As far as I was concerned, a woman like Jaclyn Love may as well have been holding a shovel, ready and willing to dig.

FOUR

JACLYN

"Girl you know I'm wanted in Canada, get that camera off me!" I fussed from behind the counter at *Dreamery* at Joia, who laughed, because she thought I was playing.

I had an unhealthy obsession with Drake a few years back, don't judge me.

Actually... hell, *I* judge me for that, so whatever.

"I have a *big* following at Blakewood," Jo reminded me, *not* lowering camera – her cell phone. In fact, she framed the two of us on the screen, making duck lips at herself as cartoonized flower crowns appeared on our heads. "If I tell them to come eat at *Dreamery*, they're coming."

"Fuck those kids," I countered, flashing a smile at her screen so she would take the picture and leave me alone. "I had to close down for two days and miss classes to restock because their hungry asses ate me out of everything in here."

Joia looked up from examining our ussie to frown. "That's not a good thing?"

"Maybe on the surface, but *Dreamery* isn't big enough to handle influencer-sponsored crowd sizes. I only have four employees, and hell, just the five of us is damn near half-capacity for this space."

"Sounds like you need a bigger space," Joia mused. "Maybe closer to campus."

"I'm perfectly happy where I am. Now, if you're not going to actually help, could you at least be quiet? I was supposed to pick where I served this community service days ago, and I just realized these spots are limited."

Finally, she put the phone down, giving me her full attention. "Sorry. We cute though."

"Duh."

"Anyway, so... limited? Meaning?"

"Meaning, there are other people who have community service to do too, and the list the judge gave me – I meant to research everywhere, and then pick a place, but then I got sidetracked."

"With Miss Thing," Joia correctly assumed, her lips curving into a smile. "I still cannot believe your ass is a cat lady now."

I raised a finger. "You mean *for* now. She can kick it with me until she's healed or whatever but then she gotta go."

"Jac, you bought that cat a bougie ass collar with her name embroidered on the bow."

I shrugged. "And? Can't I help another bitch feel good about herself after she been through something traumatic?"

"I'm *not* about to deal with you Jac," she laughed. "You know that cat ain't going nowhere."

"What I *know* is your ass keeps distracting me," I countered. "I'm out of time to research, so I've been calling each one as I have time, and their volunteer positions are filled."

Joia's eyebrow went up. "Volunteer? Girl your ass is a *criminal.*"

"A criminal *mastermind* hoe, get it right," I laughed. "Although this was *not* my finest work."

"Understatement. How are you *dealing*, anyway?" Jo asked. "Like, I know you're the baby thug of the family and all, but seriously, this has to be rough. You were already crazy busy, and now an ugly breakup, getting arrested, *community service*. How are you not curled up in a ball somewhere right now?"

I blew out a sigh and shook my head. "I don't have time to break down, as much as I might want to. This is my last semester of school, and if I mess it up, that's time and money down the drain. So I am stuffing all that emotional shit in a teensy tiny box to be packed away and opened later, at some undisclosed time. Or never. Never works."

"That sounds *super* healthy," Joia drawled, twisting her lips at me. "You need to talk to somebody. You can't neglect your mental health."

I scoffed. "I'm *not*. I read a whole article about it. An article that said pets were great for mental health."

"So you admit the cat is your pet now?"

"*Don't* put words in my mouth," I told her. "And *stop* distracting me. I can't find my list, and I *need* to do this."

"It's under your laptop."

I frowned. "What?"

"The paper you're looking for," Joia explained. "You can't see it from where you are, but it's right there under your laptop. That's why you can't find it."

I dropped my gaze to where my laptop was open on the counter in front of me, and used one hand to lift it up. Sure enough, the list I needed was underneath. I held it up, and Joia reached over the counter to take it from me.

"I knew you said you had community service but *four hundred* hours of it? Harsh."

"Nah," I shook my head. "I would've gotten jail time if Vic hadn't dropped the charges. The community service is purely punitive, cause the judge is tired of me. *Jaclyn Love, you been in and out of here too much over the last ten years. I don't wanna see you again!*" I mimicked.

Her eyes went wide. "Wow, it's that same lady from juvie court?!"

"*Mmmhmm.* And I am not trying to find out what happens if I don't get one of these 'volunteer' spaces. Read the next name to me so I can look up their number."

Joia sucked in a breath. "Uh, you know there's only one more name on this list you haven't already crossed off, right?"

I froze, my fingers poised over my keyboard. "Wait, *seriously?*"

"Yeah. *Blakewood Animal Clinic.*"

My fingers automatically pecked at the keys, typing it in. It wasn't until I hit the *enter* key that those words sank in, and a picture of the clinic façade filled my computer screen.

"Oh you gotta be fuckin' kidding me."

*W*ork for Kadan Davenport, or go to jail?
Go to jail, or work for Kadan Davenport?
Shit.

I didn't like the sound of *either* of those options, but only one of them was an option at all. Even though I knew I was pushing it by not rushing to get that volunteer position before someone else snatched it up, I couldn't bring myself to move any faster than a slow trudge down the street.

I did *not* wanna do this shit.

I lingered at the front door as long as I could without looking like a creep, then pulled the door open. Like the last time I was here, Char was at the front desk, in scrubs covered in smiling gray kittens today.

She looked adorable.

"Jaclyn!" she gushed. "How are you? Everything okay with... did you name her yet?"

I glanced around the waiting room, trying not to let my disgust show on my face as I took in these strangers and these animals and their ailments.

Swallowing the nervous lump in my throat, I nodded as I made my way to the counter. "Yes, actually. *Miss Thing*. She's doing well."

"That's great to hear! But if that's the case, how can I help you?"

I cleared my throat, leaning in so I could talk to her in a lowered tone. "Well, I have um... some community service hours I need to—"

"*Oh thank God,*" Char blurted, her fluffy natural hair bouncing around her shoulders as she clapped her hands together. "You want to do it here?"

My lip curled. "Well, that's not *exactly*... I mean yes. *Yes*. Please tell me that's still an option?"

"Of course it's an option! Or I'll make them make it an option. Come on back, I'll get Kadan!"

She motioned for me to come around the corner, and I grudgingly followed her directive, trailing her to what appeared to be a breakroom. She sat me down at a table, still bubbling with excitement as she disappeared, presumably to find Kadan.

I was bubbling too.

Well... my guts were.

It didn't take long before I felt Kadan's presence in the doorway, making my stomach twerk even harder. Reluctantly, I dragged my gaze to where he was standing, his wide frame taking up the whole entry.

Arms crossed.

Smirking.

Handsome as shit.

Bastard.

"Why is it *not* remotely surprising to me that you have to do community service?" he asked, his biceps flexing against the arms of his scrubs as he shifted. "Got something to do with the police picking you up outside my building that night?"

I sucked my teeth. "That's none of your business."

"It is though, since I'm the one with the authority to sign your paperwork," he countered, finding more smugness from somewhere. "What did you do? Let me guess – assault and battery."

"*No*," I rolled my eyes. "It was just a little body work on my ex's car. Much less than he deserved, actually. He got off easy."

Kadan scoffed. "What, he hurt your feelings? Caught him texting his side chick?"

"Side *wife*. And kids," I corrected.

"Oh. Damn."

"Yeah. So about that volunteer position?"

He nodded, stepping into the breakroom to lean against the counter that housed the microwave and coffee maker. It had been about a week since my first visit here, and his bruise was mostly gone now.

"Yeah, about that," he said, stroking a hand over his beard. "Be real with me – why here? This your last resort or something?"

"Hell yes, that's the *only* reason I'm here," I admitted. "You think I *wanted* to see your ass again? No offense."

Kadan chuckled. "Oh, trust me – that disdain you feel is mutual. But we could use the help around here. Char is overworked, and needs the relief at the front desk, so I'm not going to turn you down."

My eyes widened. "So I can have the volunteer position?"

"As long as you keep your ass away from me as much as possible, fine. How many hours?"

"I can manage ten to fourteen hours a week," I said immediately, knowing it off top since I'd already spent time working out possible schedules in my head, before I even knew where I'd be.

He nodded. "Cool, but I meant in total – meaning, how many hours do you have to give?"

"Oh. Four hundred."

Immediately, Kadan's eyebrows mashed together in a frown. "*Four hundred*? What the hell did you do to that man's car?!"

"It's not that much, not when you think about it..."

"Four hundred hours is fifty full work days!"

I shrugged. "What can I say, I'm kind of a big deal around the courthouse."

"You're serious right now?" Kadan asked, eyes wide, and I couldn't do anything except nod.

"I got in trouble as a teenager," I explained. "And then more trouble. And then a little more. And a few more times, but I've put all that behind me, and I'm an upstanding citizen now."

He let out this laugh that was somewhere between a scoff and a snort. "Oh yeah, I can see your growth between now and when you assaulted me in the middle of the night."

"I'm *sorry* about your eye, okay?" I told him, more concerned now with getting my paperwork signed to confirm my position and cover my ass. I pulled the folder I'd brought with me from my bag, rifling through to find the initial form I needed filled out. "And your dick too. It seems to be healing nicely – your eye, not your dick. I can't see your dick. I don't *want* to see your dick."

He frowned. "What's wrong with my dick?"

"Nothing's wrong with your dick, it's a nice dick," I said, still searching for the form. "A blue-ribbon dick, if you will."

"Blue-ribbon?"

I sighed. "Yes, like prize-winning. Keep up, damn."

"What am I keeping up with?" he asked, brows furrowed in confusion. "Was there a competition?"

"The Dicklympics, Kadan, *duh*."

"The *what*?!"

I looked up from what I was doing, form in hand as I did a quick mental replay of the last minute or so of conversation.

"Never mind. I've said too much."

He shook his head, approaching the table where I was sitting. "Nah, you haven't said *nearly* enough," he countered.

"Here's what I need you to sign," I said, intent on shifting the conversation away from my ridiculous musings and back to the matter at hand. "Oh, I've got a pen for you too."

"I've got my own pen," he said, pulling one from the pocket of his scrubs.

It was covered with puppy face emojis.

Cute.

"Where am I supposed to sign?" he asked, leaning over the table, so close I could smell the antibacterial soap on him, and that was the moment I *knew* I was on some bullshit, cause...

He kinda smelled good to me.

"Uh, right here," I pointed, trying my best not to inhale as I watched him read the text that was there before simply signing his name to it.

The way he was bent over the table had his ass sitting *just* right in those scrubs. The hand that wasn't holding the pen was pressed against the table, his bicep flexing under his weight. I didn't look away as his head turned in my direction, that vaguely-present bruise around his eye giving him a little ruggedness as he looked at me, running his tongue over perfect lips before he smirked.

In different circumstances, I'd give him *all* the pussy.

Like... all of it.

So much pussy.

"I guess I don't have to ask about a background check, huh? I already know your ass is a criminal," he laughed, reminding me of what the circumstances were. "You just like to tear shit up, right? Not steal? You're not gonna be swiping credit cards, are you?"

"Ha-ha," I said, drily, as I took the signed form from his hands. I stood as I returned it to the folder, and he straightened up. "I'm not a scammer."

"Tell me anything, Ms. Love."

I huffed. "It's the truth! I don't *steal*."

"Good. *Buy* scrubs to wear while you're at the front desk,

before you come back. Report to Char, and she'll show you the ropes," Kadan told me, then turned to walk off.

"Wait!" I called after him. "That's just it? That's all?"

He turned back to me, eyebrow raised. "Did you expect a welcome party or something?"

"*No*. I just... thank you, is all."

He nodded. "You're welcome. Don't make me regret it... *more*," he added, with another smirk as he walked off.

Which, I got where he was coming from, but could a bitch get credit for changing her ways?

... from a few weeks ago...?

With a heavy sigh, I returned the folder to my bag, happy I'd at least accomplished *that*. Now, I had to get back to *Dreamery* to help with the last nightly rush and close up, finish up my homework, tend to Miss Thing, wash my ass, eat some kind of dinner, and *maybe* get a few hours of sleep before my first class in the morning.

But at least the form was signed.

And only four hundred more hours of Kadan Davenport to go.

FIVE

KADAN

"Ahhhh!" I growled in some kid's face as I smacked his shot out of range of the basketball hoop he was aiming for. Of course, "kid" was a relative term, one I bestowed on anyone who seemed younger than twenty-five, which he did. He was technically an adult, but as the confidence he'd worn when he first took the shot melted into dismay at the realization I'd gotten that shit outta here, he looked like a kid ready to run home crying to his mama.

I *loved* that shit.

He was still standing there, mouth open, shocked he had *not* sunk the winning shot when I clapped him on his shoulder for one last taunt, just because he and his equally young teammate had been so confident in winning our two-on-two battle.

I looked him right in his eyes, then looked to his teammate, making sure they were both paying attention before I spoke.

"Guys," I started, my expression solemn. "I gotta say... wow, you suck. Better luck next time."

Behind me, my own partner, Jason, busted out laughing, and I joined, neither of us giving a shit about the wounded frustration on those kids' faces as they skulked off. Before the game, and through the whole first half, we'd been fifty different kinds of "old niggas at the gym", and the BC powder, IcyHot, and even PTSD jokes had been flying left and right. And this was *after* we'd had to convince them to even play against us – they had this massively incorrect idea that playing against Jay wouldn't be fair, because of his prosthetic.

They thought it was a disadvantage.

We'd enjoyed the hell out of proving them wrong.

"I would've tried to put money on it if I'd known we were gonna do 'em like that," Jay laughed, as we headed to the community center locker room. We met up here at least once a week, as part of a local veterans' group. We'd known of each other vaguely as kids, by virtue of growing up in the same town, going to the same schools. Jay was a couple of years younger than me, but I graduated the same year as one of his brothers, Justin.

"Easy money," I agreed. "Youngins never learn."

Jay and I were only in our early thirties, but to these – goddamn – college kids, that was old. They thought their twenty-year-old knees were superior, and hell, maybe they were. But the *fact* was that Jay and I – along with a few other guys our age sometimes – regularly beat the brakes off these young cats on the court.

At his locker, Jay pulled out his phone, chuckling at something on the screen. "Ay, didn't you tell me before you were trying to find ice cream you could have without fucking your stomach up?"

"I remember my stomach being fucked up and almost clearing out the whole gym behind an ice cream cone, yeah," I laughed, pulling my own bag out.

"Pretty sure they had to fumigate this place behind your funky ass," he jeered from across the aisle. "You need to see somebody about that, it ain't normal."

"You gonna tell me why you brought this up, or roast me?"

He laughed. "Both. My old lady is on it with the pregnancy cravings, wants me to grab her some ice cream from this place down the street. My cousin owns it – the *Dreamery*."

"I've heard of that," I told him. "With the gourmet flavors and shit."

"Yeah. She's got something for any food sensitivity. I was gonna see if you wanted to roll down here with me."

I frowned. "Nigga are you asking me on an ice cream date?"

He sucked his teeth. "Is this the thanks I get for trying to put you on something new? Just trying to keep you from polluting the city, bruh."

"Wow, this might be the most considerate thing you've ever done – my draws thank you," I chuckled, hooking the strap of my gym bag over my shoulder.

Jay closed his locker. "You rolling or not?"

"Yeah, I'm in," I said. "Your treat, right?" I asked, following him out.

"Why the hell would you think that?"

"You asked me on the date, you pay."

He sucked his teeth. "You not even my type."

"I'm light-skinned with a beard, I'm *everybody's* type."

I, admittedly, had a bit of a sweet tooth, so I was a little excited at the prospect of finding gourmet-quality ice cream I could enjoy without my stomach bouncing right to left to do the shoulder lean.

It was a pretty ass day outside too – sun shining, birds chirping, all that. I'd gotten in some good cardio on the court, had made those dudes feel bad about themselves – it was a *great* day.

And then I walked into *Dreamery*.

There she was behind the counter, her locs tucked away underneath a vibrantly printed headwrap that popped against her deep brown skin. Big flat wooden disc earrings hung from her ears, swinging as she turned to greet her customers – us. Her fuchsia-painted lips curved into a big, pretty ass smile – maybe my first time seeing that, and *damn*.

She looked like the afrocentric answer to everything that ailed me, especially as my eyes traveled lower, taking in the way she filled out the simple dress she was wearing.

"*Jay*," she greeted, still wearing the big smile I now understood was for him. "I already have Reese's pint of honey lavender swirl packed up and ready." Her gaze skirted past him, landing on me, and that smile fizzled as her nose curled, just a little. "*You*."

Jay's eyebrows shot up as he glanced back, looking between me and her. "Y'all know each other?"

"Oh that's right," I said, stepping forward. "You've been away from the gym the last few weeks – this woman broke into my apartment in the middle of the night and hit me in the eye."

"And the dick!" she chimed. "Don't forget I hit you in the dick too. And I did not *break in*." She shifted her attention to

Jason. "He's subletting from Jemma, and I didn't know. I tried to go spend the night there after things blew up with Victor, and here he comes. *In the damn way.*"

Jay held up his hands. "Wait a minute, the night things blew up with Victor... you mean the night I came to bail you out? That *same* night?"

"It wasn't on purpose," she whined, taking on a tone – and pouting expression – I'd never seen from her, and never would've expected.

He chuckled. "Yeah, I would guess not, but you didn't mention any of that part at all."

She shrugged. "By the time you got me out, I was exhausted," she explained. "That was a rough night."

"That's a fuckin' understatement," Jay laughed.

I took another step into the shop, which was empty except for us at this time of day. "Why do I feel like I'm missing an important, but necessary bit of context here?"

"Why do *I* feel like that applies to most parts of your life?" Jaclyn replied, smirking as she crossed her arms.

I shook my head. "Yo, you've got a *lot* of animosity to be the one that gave *me* a black eye because of your own mistake."

"You told people I was homeless, accused me of trying to eat a live animal, and called me a criminal."

"Two of those things are true though!" I countered, while Jay laughed in the background.

"Man," He chimed in. "All that happened in one night?"

Jaclyn huffed. "*No.* Over like the last few weeks. I found an injured cat on my fire escape, took it to the closest animal clinic and there his ass was again. *In the way.*"

"The same cat you've got walking around with that big ass obnoxious bow on?" Jay asked, and my eyes went wide.

"You put a *bow* on her?"

Ignoring me, Jaclyn focused on Jay. "When the hell did you see that?"

"One of Joia's vlogs. Reese plays them on the big screen."

"I'm gonna whoop her ass, I told her not to be putting me in her videos!"

Jason smirked. "*You* aren't there. *Miss Thing* is though."

"You named her *Miss Thing*? Where the hell did you get *that* from?"

This time, she acknowledged me. "I named her after Whitley from–never mind. It's not your business *anyway*. Why are you even here?"

"I brought him here," Jay cut in, "thinking I was getting you a new customer, but I see I came to get a show instead. This is entertaining as hell."

Jaclyn sucked her teeth. "I'on know why. Take this nigga on somewhere."

"You should be a whole lot nicer to me, considering I'm going to be your boss ten to fourteen hours a week," I reminded her, approaching the counter.

She pulled that pretty ass face of hers into a scowl, her eyes flashing with annoyance behind her black framed glasses. "Ten to fourteen hours of *hell*," she corrected. "And it hasn't started yet, so I'll talk to you however I want."

"Wait," Jason interjected. "What's this part about?"

"Oh I can answer this one," I said. "This woman came to me begging for a volunteer position where she can work out *four hundred* hours of community service, and I was kind enough to say *yes*. To her criminal ass."

Jason choked. "*Four hundred*. Damn, Jac, they got you like that?!"

Her expression grim, Jaclyn nodded. "Yeah, they got me like that. But this is the *last* time I get in trouble."

"You said that the *last* time you got in trouble," Jay told her, bringing that pout back to her face. "Nah, put your lip up, cousin," he laughed, turning that pout to a smile.

There's the context I was looking for.

"I'm serious this time," she said, still smiling, but with a certain seriousness to her voice. "I've got too much riding on all this to mess it up any more than I already have. I've gotta make Aunt Priscilla proud."

"Don't start no shit now," Jay told her, but gave her a nod, exchanging some type of secret cousin code, or something, I guessed.

"*Fiiine*," she agreed. "Let me grab Reese's order so you can go on about your day. And take this person with you."

Again, Jay shook his head, chuckling. "Man... you know me and Reese used to go at it like that."

Jaclyn stopped moving, her brows pulling together into a deep crease as she frowned. "Go at it like *what*?"

"Like *y'all*," Jay countered, very matter-of-fact. "A whole lotta back and forth, fussing and shit, when really..."

"Nah," I spoke up. "Nah. No. Nope. None of that."

"Whatever you say man, just calling it like I see it."

Jaclyn cleared her throat. "Yeah, now *see* your way outta here."

"Hold up," Jay said. "We can't order too?"

"Tell me what you want and then get the hell outta here you are stressing me out," Jaclyn answered him, eyes narrowed, the words spilling out so fast there was no space between them. "Well, I already know you want butter pecan like your mama," she told Jay, the smile returning to her face. "What about you?"

My gaze moved to the lines of ice cream under the glass, in frosted containers, as she moved to fix Jay's order. "Jay said you have dairy free options – which ones are those?"

"They're the ones that say *'dairy free'* on that little tag that names the flavor," she answered, in an overly sweet tone that clearly told me I was being mocked.

I really hadn't seen that until she said something though, my bad.

"Okay, I'll do the pistachio vanilla crunch. In the dairy free option."

"The full milk option?" she asked, smirking as she handed Jay his ice cream, then picked up another cup to start mine. "Add whipped cream on top?"

"Very funny," I said, as she lowered a fresh scoop toward the appropriate canister. "Actually, hold on... do I want the salted caramel instead? Or the apple pie?"

Her eyebrows went up. "I don't know, *do* you?"

"Yeah... do the salted caramel. Wait! Nah... yeah... the salted caramel. Actually..."

"You've got like two seconds before I—"

"I'll do the pistachio. Yeah. Definitely the pistachio."

She fixed her gaze on me. "You *sure?*"

"Yes."

She hesitated for a moment, then went ahead and scooped, fixing my order before I could change my mind again, and handing it to me.

"What I owe you cousin?" Jay asked, and Jaclyn flashed him another smile.

"After you got me out of the pokey at four in the morning? Please. I can't take your money Jay."

He raised an eyebrow. "Aiight now, I don't turn down free

shit."

"Our parents raised us better than to do that," Jaclyn laughed, picking up the pint of ice cream for Reese to hand to Jay. "Tell my Reesie I'm coming to see her this weekend."

"Will do," Jay nodded, turning to leave, with me right behind him.

"Um, *excuse me*," Jaclyn's voice rang out, stopping us in our tracks to turn back in her direction. "I said I couldn't take *his* money. I ain't said nothing about *yours*."

Jason burst into a cackle as he headed out the door and on about his day, leaving me to deal with his evil ass cousin. She was utterly pleased with herself as she rang me up, and I happily paid, because I knew something she didn't.

Today was the day for the weekly deep cleaning of the cages at the clinic. *Somebody* was going to have to get down and scrub all kinds of bodily fluids and hair from the floors, and we had a brand-new volunteer starting in just a few hours.

This was going to be *great*.

Jaclyn handed me my receipt with a flourish, and in return, I gave her a big smile.

"Ms. Love... I'll see you later this evening."

Something wasn't right.

So *not* right I couldn't even properly enjoy the vengeance aspect of making Jaclyn clean those cages – though her gagging and complaining were vaguely satisfying, from what I *could* hear.

When my stomach wasn't krumping.

It only seemed to get worse and worse as I worked through

the days' patients, struggling to keep my composure. I was busy trying to remember if I'd accidentally asked for cheese or something on my sandwich at lunch, when something else occurred to me.

The ice cream shop.

"Oh she's *for real* petty," I muttered to myself, holding my stomach as it complained yet again, about what I now suspected was an abundance of unauthorized dairy consumption. Well... there wasn't shit to suspect. These bubbling guts were familiar as hell.

And there was no doubt in my mind she'd done that shit on purpose.

This was too far.

You don't get a nigga back like *that*.

Once the last patient had left for the day, I went up to the front desk, catching Jaclyn there alone. Char had been excited about how easily Jaclyn picked up the front desk procedures – probably because she was a business owner herself – and had been glad for the chance to leave earlier than usual, knowing Jaclyn had the basics under control.

I was glad too.

I didn't need any collateral damage from what was about to happen.

"You ain't right, you know that?" I asked, crossing my arms as I posted up in the entryway that led to the desk.

Jaclyn looked up from what she was doing to narrow her eyes at me. "What are you talking about?"

"I feel like you know."

"I feel like this is a stupid conversation. I'm about to go home after I finish the paperwork for the new dog that came in today, but I need you to sign off on my hours, before you forget."

I smiled. "Oh, so you have a few more minutes to be here at the desk then, huh?"

Her eyebrow lifted. "Um... yeah?"

"Perfect."

Still smiling, I turned right there in the door and farted, long and hard and loud, letting out all the gas I'd been struggling to hold for the last hour while my stomach danced the macarena.

"*Oh My God!*" Jaclyn shrieked, rolling backward as far as she could in the office chair. "What the *fuck,* Kadan?!"

I shrugged, wrinkling my nose. "If I have to suffer, so do you – you're the one that did this shit to me. Damn, that's *bad* too."

Across the small space, Jaclyn gagged, pulling her shirt up over her nose. "What the hell do you mean I did this to you?!" she asked, her voice muffled by the fabric covering her mouth.

"Don't try to play dumb – oh, here we go again," I grunted, letting loose when the urge hit me again.

"I cannot. I *cannooooottt,*" Jaclyn shrieked, standing up to pace around as she coughed. "Move, let me out of here!"

"Oh we ain't going nowhere sweetheart – this is what happens when a customer asks you for dairy free, but you let petty win. Damn – here comes another one, you might wanna take cover."

"You think *I* did this?" she asked, between dry heaves, as she leaned over the desk into the waiting area, trying to gasp for fresh air. "Why would I?!"

"The same reason your ass has done *anything,*" I countered. "And I don't think, I know. I should sue your ass for poisoning me."

"Okay hold up!" she urged, holding up her hands as I farted, yet again. "Oh my *God,* that sounded so wet, *ugggh.*"

I frowned a little. "Yeah, I got a lil concerned at the end of that one, but it does me so much good to know you're smelling this too."

"I would *not* have given you the wrong ice cream on purpose!" she defended, still coughing and trying to wave away the rotten smell. "If anything, your indecisive ass confused me!"

"Oh so it's *my* fault?!" I asked. "Aiight." Her eyes went wide as I stalked toward her, turning right in her direction to let out yet another round of gas as she tried to get away, out the door.

But this was *easily* the worst one.

I blocked the door as she coughed and gagged, complaining of feeling light-headed.

"Oh my *God*, did something die in you?!" she whined, collapsing into her seat when I wouldn't let her out the door.

"Yeah. *Joy*. Because you tricked me."

"I did *not* trick you."

"So you say."

"Because that's what happened!" she insisted, coughing again as she slumped in the chair, defeated.

Mission accomplished.

She flinched as I approached the desk, but I moved past her, grabbing a pen to sign my initials on the schedule she needed for her community service.

"It was great working with you today Ms. Love," I told her, words she met with rolled eyes. "Flip the lock on your way out."

SIX

JACLYN

"So you becoming one of them lesbians now?"

"Donny! I told your ass not to say that!"

"I'm a grown ass man, Josephine, I done seen too much to not say what I got to say while I can still say it. You not about to silence me, woman!"

"It's offensive, fool!"

"I ain't said nothing was wrong with being a lesbian, I just asked if she was one! Now if *you* think lesbian is an insult, that sounds like a personal problem to me. Check your implicit biases, Josephine."

"You keep ya ass off the social medias, how about that?"

"So I won't be able to tell you how problematical you are? I see right through ya damn agenda woman."

"I got ya damn agenda Donny, kiss my *problematic* ass."

"Put it up here, I will, don't you test me girl."

What the hell is happening right now? I thought, raising an eyebrow at my cell phone screen as my parents continued their back and forth, both knowing damn well they'd be all over each other as soon as this video call ended.

Miss Thing sauntered up to me on the couch, stretching her furry orange and white body before she made the quick leap onto the seat beside me to peer into the camera too.

"*See there*?!" my father bellowed, his eyes lighting up like he'd answered some impossible question. "She got the cat all on the furniture – tell me the truth Jac, you let the cat kiss you in the mouth?"

I frowned. "What the he—*no*," I insisted, as she climbed into my lap, nuzzling her head under my chin like she was trying to make a point. "Nothing about the cat goes near my mouth."

"*That's what she said*," my father giggled, earning twin groans from me and my mother. "I thought only lesbians got cats instead of getting a man, ain't it?"

I sucked my teeth. "Daddy, you gonna act like you don't know how the *last* man I had turned out?"

"You didn't pick right."

"Wow, that's the version of this we're going with?"

"Is it a lie, Jaclyn?" He asked, eyes glittering with victory. "I'm not the one who moved in with a man with a wife and kids and dog and mortgage, so you've gotta help me out here, do I have it wrong?"

"I didn't know about *any* of that!"

My mother peered into the camera, brows drawn together in confusion. "Do you think that's a good defense? Cause it makes you sound..."

"Dumm-duh-duh-duh-dummm," my father filled in for her, cracking up at his own joke.

"Well this has been a wonderful use of my time." I quipped, and of course they laughed at that too.

"Awww, look at her face Donny I think we hurt her feelings.

We hurt your feelings sweet pea?" My mother asked, concerned.

"No," I answered her, shaking my head. None of us would've survived growing up in a house with Donald and Josephine Love without a healthy sense of sarcasm and reasonably thick skin. Between the two of them, they had jokes for everything, and there wasn't much of anything considered off-limits. "But I do have to go. This degree isn't going to earn itself, and I have work to do."

"So the graduation is on again?"

I frowned. "The graduation was *always* on. When was the graduation not on?"

"When your cousin had to go get you out of that jail for messing up that boy's car," My dad answered, wagging a finger at me. "How many times have I told you to do your drinking at home?"

"And how many times have *I* told you to always check for a camera?!" My mother added, shaking her head in disappointment. "You gotta be careful honey, you know that judge don't like you, and you *always* get her. I think she *chooses* your cases. I think she has it out for my baby. Next time, I'm gonna talk to her."

I wanted to scream, but I held it in. "There won't *be* a next time Mama," I assured her. Assured myself. "I'm done with that life. I just want to get my degree and make good ice cream."

"Yeah," My father nodded. "That judge is one fine piece of woman. Don't you worry about it Josephine, I'll have a word with her."

"So you weren't listening to me at all, huh? Cool, cool, cool," I said, at the same time my mother threatened to go upside his head.

Ten minutes later, I'd managed to get them off the phone, but my focus was shot. I leaned back into my couch cushions, only intending to rest my tired eyes for a few moments. That "few moments" flew by though, and the next thing I knew, it was dark in the apartment when I opened my eyes.

Shit.

I scrambled for my cell phone, trying to see the time. I had too much on my plate to waste hours sleeping during the day, but luckily nothing at *Dreamery* seemed to have burned down, and I hadn't had any time scheduled at the clinic today.

The only thing I'd lost was valuable schoolwork hours.

I pulled myself up from the couch to get some lights on. Late or not, the work still had to be done if I wanted to have my name called with the other non-traditional students at the graduation service.

I refilled my tumbler of water at the fridge, then headed back to my computer.

That was when I saw Miss Thing in a heap on the floor.

While she was prone to curl up and take a nap anywhere she felt like, I instantly knew something more was wrong. Her eyes were half closed, her leg in a weird position, and I don't know how, but I just felt it... she couldn't move.

"No, no no no no, nooo, *Miss Thing*," I whispered, running a hand over her head. "You're not about to do this to me honey." When I touched her, she lifted her head a little in response, letting out the weakest *meow* I'd ever heard. It made my stomach twist inside out.

I grabbed my phone to call the clinic, groaning when I realized it was already past closing. Miss Thing let out another of those pitiful sounds, making it supremely easy for me to decide my next step.

I texted Kadan.

After a few seconds of thought, I decided on...

"Hey nigga."

It didn't take long at all for him to text back.

"The fuck you want? – Dicky McStrangerballs"

I rolled my eyes, glancing at Miss Thing before I typed out a reply.

"Something is wrong with Miss Thing. She's not really moving, but she looks like she's in pain or something."

"What happened? – Dicky McStrangerballs,"

"She was like this when I woke up, so... I don't know?"

"Of course you don't. – Dicky McStrangerballs,"

"Kill the shade and just tell me what to do. Don't you care about animals?"

"I do care about animals, which is why I'm not telling YOU a thing. I know how you roll. What's your address? – Dicky McStrangerballs,"

Instead of giving in to asking him what the hell kinda rolling he thought I did, I texted him the address, letting my concern for the cat overrule my attitude. He texted that he was on his way a few moments later, and that was the first time I felt like I could breathe since I saw her on the floor.

*Bitch you **are** turning into a cat lady, wow.*

I sat there with Miss Thing until Kadan's knock sounded at the door. I wanted to take my time, and make him wait, but the cat looked so pitiful I put the petty aside to let him in.

I *realllly* wasn't expecting him to look so good.

I'd seen Kadan naked, I'd seen him dressed for work, I'd seen him after the gym. What I *hadn't* seen was this… *Netflix and Chill* Kadan, in a black tee and gray sweats and a hat pulled low over his eyes.

Dick Appointment Kadan.

At least, that's what it would've seemed like if it weren't for the medical bag in his hand.

"Where's my patient?" he asked, an additional reminder of why he was actually there that spurred me to step aside so he could come through the door.

"She's over on the floor in front of the couch," I told him, closing and locking the door as he headed in that direction. I followed, but hung back, trying to give him room to do what he needed to do, but he looked up at me like I was crazy as he knelt on the floor.

"You gonna just stand there and watch, or help me?"

My eyes went wide. "Um… help, I guess, but I have no idea what I'm supposed to do."

"Just hold her," he said. "And keep her calm."

I lowered myself to the floor and gently pulled Miss Thing into my lap. I watched, awed, as Kadan carefully examined her while speaking soft, comforting words. It was sweet the way he handled her, patiently, even when she tried to nip and scratch at him when he made it to her right hind paw.

"What the hell are you feeding her?" he asked, sitting back when he was done.

"Not that stuff you gave me. I feed her Arcana," I told him, proud of myself for having researched and found the best food.

He raised an eyebrow at me as he ran a soothing hand over Miss Thing's head. "I should have been clearer. *How much* are you feeding her is the better question. She's gained a *lot* of weight since I saw her last month."

"Happy weight," I defended, pulling her close to my chest. "Of course she gained weight, she's getting steady meals now!"

Kadan shook his head. "Too many meals. She's got a sprain, Jaclyn. Probably from moving awkwardly with a sudden increase in weight. She's used to being light on her feet, and thinks she can still move like that, but she can't. *Especially* coupled with the injury she already had."

I sucked my teeth. "It sounds to me like you have an issue with a woman with meat on her bones."

"Not at all," Kadan laughed. "I'm in full support of a healthy weight, but this is too fast of a pace. She needs to be getting more exercise – once the sprain heals – and a consistent diet, on a schedule – she shouldn't be allowed to constantly graze from a bowl that stays full all day."

I opened my mouth to deny I was letting that happen, but he looked pointedly at the – full – food bowl next to the kitchen.

"Fine," I groused. "I guess *you* don't believe thick thighs save lives either, huh?"

"Not for cats," he chuckled. "For now, she needs to rest. She likely fell, and it dazed her a bit, but she'll be fine. I'm almost positive it is just the sprain, but if she hasn't improved in a few days we can bring her in for an x-ray. Okay?"

I nodded. "Yeah. Okay."

He took Miss Thing from my arms, depositing her in the cat bed near the window. I watched as he gathered up the few things he'd taken from his medical bag and put them away, then followed him to the kitchen to wash his hands.

"Thanks for coming to check on her for me. I didn't realize a vet really *would* make an after-hours house call for free."

"Free?" he raised an eyebrow as he soaped his arms up to his elbows. "This shit wasn't free, just like that ice cream. I have every intention of taking your money."

I scoffed. "Seriously? All you did was poke her a lil bit and call her fat!"

"I diagnosed the problem." He smirked as he started rinsing away the soap, then moved aside so I could wash my hands too. "If it makes you feel better, you can give her an ice pack, but most cats won't let it stay in place anyway."

"Thanks for that," I told him, hoping he picked up on my sarcasm as I handed him a few paper towels. "Now get out."

"Damn, I don't get a tour or anything? I can't go lock myself in *your* bedroom like you did in my spot?"

"It was a misunderstanding," I defended, drying my hands. "Are we still focused on that?"

He shrugged. "Considering I was the one who left the misunderstanding with a black eye, I think we can focus on it as long as I want to."

"You *farted* on me," I countered. "Surely that's restitution enough."

"Nah, not when you're the one who gave me dairy."

"I *told you* that was a mistake! Your indecisive ass confused me!"

Kadan's eyebrow went up. "Is that how you'd defend yourself in court after giving the wrong customer peanuts? You were just *confused*?"

"So you're going to sue me now?" I asked. "That's the scenario we're working with here?"

"Nah," he shook his head. "That's not the plan."

"But there *is* a plan." My eyes narrowed at him, annoyed by his calm demeanor and handsome face. "Tell me what it is. Tell me *now*."

"I never said there was a plan."

"But clarifying that something *isn't* 'the plan' leaves a clear implication that there *is* a plan."

"I didn't say that though."

I groaned. "But you implied it!"

"Did I imply it, or did you assume? You know what they say about assuming, right?" he teased, his face pulled into an impossibly sexy, impossibly frustrating smirk.

Ughhh.

"You know I'm not scared to fight you, right?"

He laughed, and shook his head. "Yeah, actually. I do."

"Then stop playing with me!"

"Ain't nobody playing with you," he laughed harder. "Your ass is paranoid because you know you're wrong."

"I haven't done anything!"

"Your criminal record would beg to differ."

For some reason, that shit knocked the air out of my lungs.

Logically, I knew he didn't mean any harm, we were just going back and forth. But the truth was... it was embarrassing. As much as I loved myself, I wasn't even remotely proud about my past, or the fact it was documented in detail for everyone to see how much of a fuckup I was. I wanted to put it behind me. Was *trying* to put it behind me.

It felt really, really, *not* good to be reminded of it.

"Hey..."

Kadan's voice was different now, with none of the amusement from a moment ago. Quickly, I fixed my face, not wanting the hurt to show, but it was too late.

"My bad," he said, taking a step toward me. "I didn't mean to take it too far."

I shook my head. "It's fine. It's whatever," I said, even though it wasn't. I couldn't be mad though, because I'd earned my record – none of it was a lie. I *wasn't* mad.

I was disappointed in myself.

"Thank you for coming to check on Miss Thing," I said, trying to send the message it was time for him to go. "I'll make sure she rests up."

He didn't move though.

"Wow," he spoke instead. "You're for real sensitive about that, aren't you? Why?"

I frowned. "Why the hell do you care?"

"Is there something wrong with giving a shit about other people?"

"No," I answered. "But there's something *weird* about it. You don't even like me."

"I never said that, but you punched me in the eye. And kneed me in the dick."

"So we're back on that again?"

He shrugged. "It's a hard thing to forget."

"Okay so what do I have to do to get us past this, huh? Are you like a toddler or something, before you can move on, you need me to kiss it and make it better?"

His face twisted in surprise. "You offering? Cause *hell yeah*."

"I was talking about your *face*, fool!" I laughed, pushing him away as he walked up on me. "I don't want your lil raggedy dick near my mouth!"

He let out a bark of laughter. "Little? *Raggedy*?" he put a hand to his chest. "*I* recall you saying it was an award-winning dick. Gold medal dick at the *Dicklympics*."

I held up a hand. "What I *actually* said was 'blue-ribbon', please get it right."

"Gold medal, blue-ribbon, same difference. Either way, you said it then, so don't be fronting on my mans now."

"Ain't nobody fronting on you, Kadan," I laughed. "The truth of the matter is, I don't have complete information to grade your dick *anyway*."

His facial expression changed, focused. "Okay, you have my attention. What else you need?"

I crossed my arms, meeting his gaze. "Well, among my girls and I, there are three parts to the score. The look of the dick, the performance of the dick, and the *trouble* factor."

"What's the trouble factor?"

I grinned. "Whether the look and performance are worth the trouble of dealing with the person the dick is attached to."

"What's my trouble factor?" he asked, smirking.

I smirked right back at him. "I'm not fucking you, so I wouldn't know."

"But if you *were*, what would it be?"

"It's not something I can guess, dude. I don't know you like that – don't know about your unstable exes or whoever you're dealing with now, have no idea what kinda stamina you have, or what your stroke is like. Hell, I don't even have enough data for a full visual report, because you weren't hard. I don't *really* know what you're working with on any level."

Kadan scoffed. "So you spark my interest then leave me hanging. That's cold."

"Sorry Dr. Davenport, but unless you're trying to submit the incomplete data, I got nothing for you."

His eyebrows lifted, and he pulled his lip between his teeth. "So submitting the missing data *is* an option?"

I raised my shoulders, just slightly. "I *am* always interested in qualitative research. For the good of humanity, you know?"

"Absolutely," he nodded, closing the distance between us again. He put his hands on the counter on either side of me, boxing me in. "Who am I to get in the way of your pursuit of the greater good?"

I grinned as I tipped my head back, looking into his face. His eyes were shadowed with lust, enough to make my thighs clench. "Are we doing this?"

He leaned in, bringing his face toward mine. "You tell me..."

"Nah," I said. "*You* tell *me*," I countered, slipping my hands between us, into the waistband of his sweats. I cupped him through the soft fabric of his boxers, grinning in his face as he grew harder – and bigger – in my hand.

"*Hell yes,*" he growled, prompting me to let out a squeal as he grabbed and picked me up. I wasn't anybody's definition of dainty, but he hooked my legs around his waist with ease, then looked me right in the face and said, "Point me to your bedroom."

So of course, I did.

"Wait, hold up!" I said, stiff-arming him once he'd dropped me onto the bed and attempted to climb on top of me. "This is *purely* for research, right? You're not going to mess around and get attached?"

He shrugged. "I won't if you won't," he answered, then pulled off his shirt and hat, tossing both aside before he went for the hem of my oversized *Blakewood* tee. I let him strip me down to nothing, and then while he was getting rid of the rest of *his* clothes, rummaged around in my nightstand for condoms.

Couldn't conduct an experiment without the proper precautions.

After donning the condom, Kadan spread my legs wide, positioning himself between them before he sank in. I gripped handfuls of my sheets as he lowered his chest to my breasts, and his mouth to mine.

I hadn't expected kissing to be a part of the plan.

But as soon as his lips touched mine, I was glad for them. They were as perfectly kissable as I'd expected, and he was good at it. *Really* good.

A low moan escaped my throat as he stroked me deep, matching the movement with his tongue in my mouth. One of his hands tangled in my locs, the other kept a handful of my ass in his grip as he moved, creating a steady pace of sweet friction.

I hooked my arms around his neck, rolling my hips with his, matching his pace as he stroked. And we kissed.

Deeper.

Faster.

Harder.

Those kisses came to an end as he sat back to hook my knees over his arms, spreading me open wide to go *even* deeper, *even* harder. My hands went to my breasts, cupping and squeezing my sensitive flesh as orgasmic pressure built in my core. His hands moved to my ankles, holding my feet high in the air as he plunged into me.

Deeper.

Faster.

Harder.

Until I came unglued, with a loud, keening cry I didn't care if my neighbors heard.

They'd deal.

Kadan didn't stop, still chasing his nut even as I came down from mine. He kept stroking, kept pounding, kept the waves of orgasm on a steady reverb through my legs as he kept moving, until he suddenly stopped, mouth wide open.

"*Ahhh shit!*" he yelled – *screamed* –loud as shit, as he collapsed to his elbows on top of me. I turned away, pressing my lips together as a laughed bubbled up from my stomach.

Jac... do not laugh in this dude's face.

"Goddamnit. *Goddamnit*," he groaned, in a strained voice that brought tears to my eyes. "Jaclyn please...*the cat...*"

I knew my pussy was good, but how in the world was I ever going to look him in the eyes again, knowing *this* was how he acted when he got some?

"*The cat... Jac... please...*," he begged, looking me right in the face, with glossy eyes.

"Damn," I blurted, before I could help myself. "Is it *that* good to you?"

"What? *No!*" he hissed, through gritted teeth. "The *cat*, Jaclyn. Miss Thing!"

I frowned. "*What?!*"

"She..." he blew out a deep, shaky breath. "She... she has... her claws in my ass."

As if she'd been waiting on her cue, Miss Thing hissed, announcing her presence in the room.

Well she'd already announced herself to Kadan, but I guess now it was time to let *me* know too.

Now that I understood why he was holding himself like a statue, I maneuvered from underneath him to see what the hell was going on. I flipped on the overhead fixture to give better light than what was coming from the lamp, and sure enough Miss Thing had latched herself to Kadan's ass.

I couldn't help it.

I laughed.

"*Can you get the cat off me!?*" he screeched, his voice in such a higher pitch than normal it made me laugh even harder between trying to soothe Miss Thing enough to carefully unhook her claws from Kadan's flesh.

"You know she did this to you cause you called her fat, right?" I asked, still struggling to keep myself together as I successfully removed her from his ass. It was a good thing he hadn't tried to snatch her off – he only had the holes from where she pushed her claw in now, but any sudden attempt to remove her would have made it much, much worse.

"She did this because you were moaning and hollering like I was killing you," he countered, out of breath, as he collapsed fully onto the bed. "*Fuck.*"

I kept right on chuckling as I deposited Miss Thing back in her designated spot, gave her a treat, then headed back to my bedroom, closing the door after myself this time.

"You know this shit ain't funny right?!" Kadan complained as I stepped into my bathroom to wash my hands.

"The hell it aint!" I called back. Once my hands were clean, I grabbed my first aid kit and went back to the doorway, holding it up. "You look like you could use some *ass*-sistance," I teased, drawing his gaze to where I was standing.

"Ms. Love, can you please quit playing and get your fine ass over here and patch me up?" he asked, his eyes doing an appreciate sweep over my nude body.

I smirked. "Oh I'm *fine* now?"

"*Been* fine. Now please? I'm bleeding out."

"You are *not* bleeding out," I laughed, when I got back to him to look at those tiny pinpricks again.

Okay, they were a little bigger than pinpricks, but still.

"How are you a whole doctor – albeit an animal doctor – acting like a whole baby over this?" I asked, kinda enjoying the view as I used alcohol pads to clean his wounds. His ass was nice and muscled, probably why Miss Thing's attack hurt so bad, not enough soft fat to cushion the blow.

"Tease me all you want, that shit felt like taking shrapnel to the ass. That sprain must not be hurting her *too* badly."

I laughed. "You wanna tell me how you know what shrapnel feels like?"

"Cause I've felt shrapnel," he quipped back. "You see the tattoos, right?"

I had, but hadn't *really* looked at them. Now I did, noting here and there that the ink mimicked some I'd seen on Jay, who was also a veteran.

"*Oh.* Wow..." I mused, tracing one on his back I recognized as a medical symbol. "That's where you got involved in medicine I guess?"

"Yep. Worked my way up to medic, then got the hell outta there cause I was tired of seeing people die. Not that seeing animals die is a piece of cake, but..."

"Hits different. Yeah, I would imagine so."

I finished bandaging both his ass cheeks, then patted him to signal that I was done. He grinned at me as he turned over.

"Yeah. That's one way to put it."

For a moment, we were both quiet, taking in and admiring the other person's nudity. He was still wearing that condom – empty, since we'd gotten interrupted – and rock hard, sticking straight up.

"I hope you're not in *too* much pain," I told him. "I'm sorry Miss Thing got protective."

66

I THINK I MIGHT LOVE YOU

He chuckled, tucking his hands behind his head – getting comfy as hell in my bed. "No you're not. Your ass was laughing."

"I'm sorry, I thought that was... I thought that was just how you sounded and acted when you came, and I'm sorry, that shit was ridiculous. No lie, I was going to roast the fuck outta you with my sisters."

"Cold world," he laughed. "Cat messed up my score."

I giggled. "No, you did good. You presented well."

"Nah, it's tainted."

My gaze shifted from his teasing eyes to his hard dick, practically begging for my attention. When I met his eyes again, it was clear he was thinking the same thing I was.

"We could always run the experiment again..." I suggested, disposing of the packaging I'd used, then utilizing a fresh wipe for my hands. "In the interest of fairness, you know?"

His eyebrows went up. "Well I'm at a disadvantage now, with the injury... unless you'd be willing to provide some sort of accommodation?" he asked, as I climbed over him.

Once I'd gotten myself perfectly in line, I looked at him with a smile.

"Oh, don't you worry about that. I've got a *long* list of alternative research methods we can work through." I sank onto him, pulling a groan from both our lips. "Let's get started."

SEVEN

KADAN

So obviously I messed up.

Bad.

And the thing was, I couldn't even blame my inability to stay *away* from Jaclyn Love – due to her volunteering at the clinic – on my inability to stay *out* of her. Nah, I walked into that with my eyes *wide* open. I saw *everything*.

Which, of course, presented a new problem.

How to keep myself from going back for more?

It was one thing when all I had against me was my imagination – the fantasy of what she looked like underneath her clothes. But now that I was intimately familiar with that soft skin, those ample curves, plush thighs, pillowy breasts, tight pu...

Damn.

She got your ass bad.

So bad I was sitting in my place on my night off, beer in hand, wings on the coffee table, NBA on the tv, but I wasn't paying attention to any of that shit.

My mind was on Jaclyn.

I'd invited her over.

Obviously, she'd said no because she wasn't here, but it had taken a lot for me to push through and even ask, mainly because my ass knew better. I didn't *need* her over here, didn't *need* her scent permeating my space, didn't *need* to get drawn further into *her*. But even with all that in mind, the rejection still stung like a bitch.

"Ms. Love... I'm sure you already know this, but thorough research involves conducting your tests more than once. Varied times, varied conditions, varied settings, all that, you know?" I was nervous enough that my palms were sweating, which was... what the fuck?

Jaclyn turned from her post at the desk with that dazzling smile, clear amusement in her eyes. "As much as I appreciate a good ongoing scenario, I unfortunately have to decline. I am insanely busy, and I kinda want to graduate in a few weeks like I'm supposed to, so I kinda have to be on sabbatical. If you catch my drift?"

Immediately, I nodded. "Absolutely. Totally get it."

"Sorry," she said, like she meant it. "You're a gold medalist though, I'm sure you can find another research partner. Easily."

She was right.

I could.

But I didn't *want* a different "research partner."

See?

See?

One night of pussy, a week ago, and she had me in my feelings.

The ringing of my cell phone snatched me from my pity

party as I reached to grab it from the table. The name on the screen brought an instant smile to my face.

"Aunt Cali," I greeted, picking up the remote to crank the volume on the TV down. "What can I do for my favorite Auntie today?"

On the other end of the line, she snickered. "Boy, I'm your *only* Auntie."

"That doesn't mean you're not my favorite."

"How could I *not* be?"

"If I didn't even like you."

That made her laugh again. "I'm a lovable person Kadan, everyone likes me."

"I can think of a large group of people who'd disagree," I countered back.

"And that's why they're where they are and I'm where I am," she said, with the signature sass that always amused the hell out of me. "Now stop getting me riled up so I can tell you this."

"Tell me what?"

"Guess who I ran into a few minutes ago?" she asked, sounding damn near giddy.

That meant it was one of my old teachers, an old classmate, or one of my old girlfriends that she managed to like.

"Uhh... Mr. Jenkins?" I said, pulling a name out of my ass, cause there were too many possibilities for me to *actually* guess.

"No! Deidre Daniels!"

Oh.

Oh.

No.

"Oh, is *that* right?" I asked, trying my best not to give even the tiniest inflection to suggest that was news I wanted to hear. Deidre Daniels didn't fall into any of the categories I'd mentioned before – she occupied the most exclusive group of all.

Women my Aunt Calista wanted me to make her pseudo-daughter-in-law.

"Yessss," Aunt Cali gushed. "And she was looking gorgeous as always. I know you remember her, don't you?"

Yes.

Yes, of course I remembered DeeDee with the double-ds.

Dee-Dee was fine as hell.

She was also *exactly* like my aunt, which was fine... for my aunt. The fancy parties and proper etiquette and high-society Black shit, that was all well and good, if that was what you were into. Deidre and Aunt Cali were *very* into it.

I was not.

Aunt Cali thought I'd never given Deidre a fair chance, but that wasn't it. Deidre and I had gotten down a bit as teenagers, before I went off to the service, and I even took a second dip when I came back. For a whole entire week, I subjected myself to her constant critique of everything from my haircut to my tats to my posture to my language to my choices at dinner to the clinic I wanted to work at. Everything was "shocking" or "disgusting" or "improper" or "ghetto", by which her ass meant "too Black."

I chose the most shocking, disgusting, improper, "ghetto" words I could string together to break *that* shit off.

I didn't need that energy.

And the thing was, I was sure she felt the same about me, but she idolized Aunt Cali, who saw *none* of those supposed flaws Deidre spent her time picking apart. Surely she saw them in others, but I was her only nephew, the treasured son of her "troubled" baby sister who was God knows where.

Between the two of them – Deidre and Aunt Calista – I was sure they thought I could be molded into their narrow definition of "Black Excellence", with a little refinement to my demeanor and appearance and job, but I was good.

I was already excellent as fuck if you asked me, but somehow no one ever did.

Damn shame.

"We should all get together for dinner soon," Aunt Cali suggested, bringing my attention away from my own musings and back to the phone. "Do some reconnecting."

Here we go.

"You know I don't get along with Deidre like that, so I can't imagine it would be a good time for anybody involved," I said, trying to put at least a *little* sugar on the fact that I couldn't stand Deidre.

Aunt Cali sighed. "You were practically still children the last time you even spoke. Surely you get along now, as adults?"

"I've interacted with her as an adult. It wasn't fun. I'll pass. But you should go, Auntie. Have a good time. And don't tell me *anything* about it."

"Kadan!" she scolded, with a huff. "I think you should reconsider. Deidre is a lovely young woman, who I'm sure would make a lovely life partner."

"For another nigga, sure."

"*Language!*"

Fucccck why did I answer this phone?

"Kadan Davenport, I am getting older," she started, and I closed my eyes, knowing where this was about to go. "I have done the best I could by you, in the absence of my sister, and now your father. Made sure you had a support system when you came back from that God-awful desert, ensured your education without any debt... you give me one *good* reason you can't indulge me in a single meal."

Shit.

Shit, shit, shit.

I just don't fucking want to wasn't going to fly, even though it was the truth.

Fine.

"I don't think my girlfriend would like it that much," I lied, using the first thing that came to mind. In my experience, if a woman wouldn't accept any other "no" for an answer, they'd at least hesitate a bit over another woman's "property".

Or so I hoped.

"*Girlfriend?!*" Aunt Cali exclaimed, and I instantly realized my mistake. I was already kicking myself, even before the, "Oh my word, when did you get a girlfriend, when were you going to tell me, who are her people, I have to meet her!" left her mouth.

That's what you get for lying.

"It's still early," I claimed, trying to backtrack. "We're not quite at *meet the family* seriousness yet, but I don't want to make her uncomfortable, knowing what your intention is for getting me and Deidre together."

Aunt Cali sighed. "Of course, I understand. You're trying to neutralize your father's negative influence by not allowing the philandering nature you inherited from him to rule you."

"Chill, Auntie," I warned. Not that she wasn't justified in her disdain for my father – his hoe antics couldn't have been particularly healthy for my mother's mental state, and as judgmental as Aunt Cali was, she was protective of her sister.

That was still my father though.

"Is that not what you're saying, Kadan? If it isn't, please explain it to me."

"I want as little drama as possible. How's that?" I asked. "Nothing to do with my father, everything to do with *me*."

"Fair enough. I want to meet this young lady. How does she feel about your work? Does she understand the altruistic appeal of it?"

"She doesn't care how much money I make," I replied, since that's what she was *really* asking. That wasn't technically a lie I guessed, since any woman I gave that title *wouldn't* be pressed about my job title.

"I didn't say anything about *money*," Aunt Cali whined, feigning offense. She may not have used that word, no, but that was the underlying question. "Does she like animals? Visit the clinic?"

"Sometimes."

"Hm," she replied, in a way that made me shake my head. Not even a whole word, just a loaded sound of disapproval from deep in her throat – the obvious implication being that an *acceptable* woman for me wouldn't deign to visit a community-sponsored animal clinic.

Or be okay with me working there in the first place.

"Kadan, you understand that I only want the absolute *best* for you, right?" she asked, like she knew she was pushing it too far. "I know you think I'm stuffy, and boring, but the truth is that your uncle and I live a good life – I want that for you as well. You're about to be thirty-five. It's *time* for you to settle with a good woman, from a good family, and—"

"I don't think we have the same definition of *good*, Aunt Cali," I interrupted her. "But I *do* believe you mean well. You just have to understand that I'm going to choose who I choose. *If I choose.*"

"Now see, you're trying to give me a heart attack now."

I chuckled. "Nah, never that. Just trying to prepare you."

"Well, will you at least be bringing her as a date to the alumni ball?"

Shit.

"I will ask her. That's all I can offer for now."

"Mmmhmmm. Well you let her know I'm looking forward to meeting her."

"Of course Auntie. Consider it done."

She spent the rest of the call inundating me with details about luncheons and alumni meetings and a bunch of other boring shit I didn't have the heart to tell her I didn't care about. But, to her credit, she was beating me down with too much information for my thoughts to return to Jaclyn... at least until we hung up the phone.

Inexplicably, I found myself wondering if Jaclyn's parents were on her ass about "settling down" – if that's why she was working so hard to finish school before summer. She was only in her mid-twenties, but I knew how the shit went for women – that was around the time they started getting the "husband and babies" pressure.

But she didn't strike me as the type to care about all that.

Actually she struck me as the type to outright reject it.

I wasn't supposed to be letting her strike me as *anything* though.

I turned off the TV and pulled myself up from the couch, intent on clearing my thoughts. A shower, then bed, then sleep, where hopefully I wouldn't encounter Jaclyn.

Or hell, Deidre.

Or hell... *both*.

I shuddered, then unlocked my cell phone to enter a search term I knew was ridiculous, but I'd take whatever advice I could get on getting my ass to sleep without dreaming.

$$\sim$$

F *uck.*
Fuuuuuck fuck fuck fuck.

I was sitting in my office at the clinic when the sound of a car drew my attention to the window. It was lucky – lucky as *hell* – that history had made me more aware of my surroundings than I might normally have been, because otherwise I might *not* have noticed my Aunt Cali stepping carefully out of her Mercedes in the parking lot of the animal clinic, stopping to check her red-bottoms before she started moving with purpose toward the building.

Hence, all those *fucks* from earlier.

I moved as fast as I could, dashing to the front desk, where Jaclyn was filing paperwork for new patients since the waiting room was quiet today.

"Hey!" I called, startling her so badly that I was met with raised fists as she turned in her chair.

"*What?!*" she snapped, pressing a hand to her chest when she realized it was me.

"I need a favor – can't explain a lot, but I need you to pretend to be my girlfriend right quick, so my Aunt doesn't try to marry me off into some Black Stepford shit."

Jaclyn's pretty face pulled into a frown. "Aren't you grown? Like grown as hell?"

"Your parents don't ever get in your shit like you're still a teenager?" I countered, peering toward the doors where Aunt Cali would be appearing any second.

"Well yeah, I guess," she admitted. "Whatever. What's in it for me?"

"I'll sign off on a weeks' worth of your volunteer hours, while you're studying, or running your business, or whatever."

Her eyebrow lifted as she smirked. "That's a crime."

"Something you're *very* familiar with," I reminded her. "We got a deal or not?"

She put her finger to her chin, looking up to the ceiling as she pretended to consider it.

While I watched Aunt Cali approach the front door.

"*Jaclyn.*"

"Fine," she chirped, wearing a big smile.

"Good, cause she's here right now," I hissed, wrapping an arm around her waist as I pretended not to see Aunt Cali coming through the door. She felt comfortable as hell against my body, at least until she glanced into the waiting room. Then, her body stiffened as she turned to look at me, eyes wide.

"*That's your auntie?!*" she half-mouthed, half-whispered. When I nodded, her eyes got even bigger. "*Bruh, trust me, this ain't the lie you wanna tell!*"

"*We have a deal!*" I shot back, then looked past her, to where Aunt Cali was standing, a pair of designer sunglasses dangling from her fingers. "*Auntie,*" I greeted. "What are you doing here?"

She didn't even hear me.

Or if she did, she didn't react – she was too focused on Jaclyn, who turned to fully face her. "*Hey Auntie,*" she quipped, putting on a big, obviously fake smile that made my Aunt's nostrils flare.

"You know this person, Kadan?" Aunt Cali asked, her jaw tight as her attention shifted to me. I knew she was going to disapprove of any girl I put in front of her that wasn't already pre-approved, but *damn*. Neon pink scrubs aside, Jaclyn "looked" the part. She was pretty as hell, well groomed, all that. My best guess was that Aunt Cali had come here *hoping* to run into my "girlfriend", and was already prepared to be an asshole to her.

The problem with that though… Jaclyn would give that asshole energy right back.

"Of course I know her," I answered, even though my gut was telling me I should choose a different course of action. That could've also been the cheese on my breakfast sandwich this morning though. "This is the woman I was telling you about a few days ago, remember?"

That constipated look on my Aunt's face deepened. "No. I don't."

"Quit it Auntie – this is Jaclyn Love. Jaclyn, this is my Aunt Calista."

Aunt Cali's nostrils flared as her eyes flashed toward Jaclyn. "Oh, Ms. Love is *quite* familiar with me. Aren't you, sweetheart?"

Beside me, Jaclyn sighed. "Hey Judge Freeman."

"Hay is for horses, young lady," Aunt Cali snapped, her tone and expression as stern as if she was on the bench, not in the waiting room at an animal clinic.

"*Hello*, Judge Freeman," Jaclyn corrected herself. "Is there something I can do for you?"

"There most certainly is not," my aunt answered.

Jaclyn's eyes went to Aunt Cali's head. "You sure? We're good with pets."

Oh, shit.

"Is this some sort of joke to you? Some twisted retribution for your sentence? You've decided to corrupt my nephew?" Aunt Calista asked, her light brown skin darkening to a fairly distinct red tint.

"She's the one who gave you that harsh ass sentence?!" I hissed in Jaclyn's ear.

"I told your ass this wasn't it. Her name was on the paper you signed!"

"I didn't actually read that shit!"

"Ahem!" Aunt Cali cleared her throat, bringing our attention back to her as she looked back and forth between us. "I'm waiting on an answer."

"*No*," Jaclyn said. "No one is trying to corrupt Kadan – I didn't even know he was your nephew. But I wouldn't be here if it wasn't for you, so thank you for putting me in his path."

My aunt made that same disgusted sound she'd made on the phone the other day, then looked to me. "Is *this* who you're bringing to the alumni ball? With her *record*? You do know she has a *record*, right?"

"I prefer to focus on the fact that she's a successful business owner, and right on the verge of a college degree," I answered. "And of course, the fact that she's gorgeous," I added, throwing syrup on it to pull my aunt's focus to Jaclyn's positive qualities, since she was apparently familiar with the other ones.

Jaclyn turned to me with a smile. "I am, huh?" she asked, pursing her lips before she lifted them, obviously prompting me for a kiss, which of course I gave.

And lingered on.

And enjoyed a little too much.

"*Well*," Aunt Cali huffed, planting her sunglasses back on

her face like she was trying to block us out. "I came here to ask you to join me for lunch, Kadan, but it seems I've lost my appetite."

"Good luck with that," Jaclyn said, before I could respond with something less antagonistic.

Aunt Cali's eyes narrowed, and she shook her head. "Kadan... we'll talk."

And then she was gone.

"That did not go like I expected it to," I said, watching Aunt Cali as she stomped off.

"Yeah," Jaclyn said, unthreading herself from my arms. "You did not think that shit through. At all."

"I didn't. *Fuck.*"

Jaclyn leaned against the front desk, arms crossed. "Yeah. *Fuck* is right. I tried to warn you when I saw her. If you'd given me a *real* heads up, I could've told you that lady cannot stand me, and now she's going to work *harder* to get you with some *Talented Tenth Barbie* bitch. Your bad."

"Do you *have* to rub it in like this?" I asked, tossing up my hands.

She laughed. "No, of course I don't *have* to, but did you think I would pass up the chance? You're still gonna sign off on my volunteer hours, right?"

"You're coming to this alumni ball, right?"

Jaclyn sucked her teeth. "Uhh, that was *not* part of the deal."

"It is now – I know I'll get left alone if you're on my arm, seeing how she feels about you. Hell, she might even uninvite me."

"*That's* fucked up," Jaclyn snapped. "But it's also my kinda shenanigans, so whatever. I'm in. You're paying for everything though – dress, makeup, shoes..."

"Cool," I agreed.

"And three weeks off, not two."

"*Fine,*" I agreed, extending my hand. "We got a deal?"

Jaclyn smiled, accepting my hand. "Yep. We got a deal."

EIGHT

JACLYN

"Hey!" I hissed into the phone. "If you have a friend who needs a job, bring them with you."

Emmi laughed as she agreed and ended the phone call, but I was deadass serious.

It was an emergency.

"Sorry about that delay," I told the next customer in the long ass line I had Joia to thank – curse out – for. She'd dropped another one of those mentions on her social media, which had people flooding to *Dreamery*, making it a much busier day than it usually would be. Which, normally, would be fine.

Not *today* though.

Today, I was paying for my hiring of a group of friends – one was pregnant, and had gone into premature labor today. It was her day off anyway though!

But.

The boyfriend/baby's father was *not* off today.

Neither was the best friend.

Guess where *none of them* were today?

At *Dreamery*.

Not that I could blame them. If the mother of my child or best friend went into labor too early, I'd be right there at the hospital too, fuck that ice cream! However, me understanding why they weren't here didn't put me in any less of a shitty predicament, when I only *had* one other employee.

Maybe I shouldn't have asked her to bring a friend, seeing how this went.

In any case, while I waited for Emmi – and a friend if I were lucky... maybe... - to arrive, it was just me, handling a growing horde of customers. Fortunately, Dreamery was adorable with it's all white and chrome interior, so plenty of people were distracting themselves with selfies and other flicks.

Which hopefully wouldn't bring in too many more people.

I had a Critical Leadership paper to finish.

I had to focus on the task in front of me though, serving the line of people at the counter properly, and with a smile. Scoop, smile, checkout, smile, send them on their way, smile. Over, and over, and over.

Until I caught sight of a familiar face in the crowd.

Ah shit.

The last thing I had time for right now was going back and forth with Kadan Davenport, but there he was anyway, a cocky smirk on his face as he sauntered past the line.

"*What the hell are you doing?*" I hissed at him as he came behind the counter, right up to me.

"You look like you could use help," he said, just loud enough for me to hear it. "So, tell me what I'm doing."

I narrowed my eyes. "You're helping me?"

"Why is that so surprising?"

"Why *wouldn't* it be?"

"Your customers are waiting," he reminded me, forcing me

back to the reality of my situation. Emmi wasn't here yet, and that line was getting longer.

"Fine," I told him. "Scrub your hands, put on a hairnet and apron, and put on gloves."

Not even ten minutes later, I felt decidedly less frazzled, with Kadan at my side scooping up ice cream. He was a little slow, because he didn't know the layouts like I did, but he still kept the line moving – and did a nice amount of upselling too. We fell into a rhythm, and by the time Emmi arrived it was a lot less chaotic than it had been when I called her, frantic.

And she *did* bring a friend.

She took over while I gave her friend a quick lesson on serving the ice cream, and signed a little paperwork. At first, I thought Kadan had disappeared on me once my reinforcements arrived, but a scan of the shop showed me he'd stepped out to clear the tables and floor of discarded cups and napkins, and chat with my customers a bit.

How is everything about this man a turn-on?
Seriously.

Who the hell looks good in a hairnet and apron?
Kadan Davenport, that's who.

He was lowkey – highkey – sexy as usual, in sweats and a tee shirt under the apron. He was wearing that hat again too, and his silly ass had pulled the hairnet over it.

Still fine as hell.

I'd called to leave a message with Char that I wouldn't make it to the clinic today, because of the fiasco with the shop. I didn't think Kadan was even on staff for the day, but I was sure the message had gotten back to him. He'd probably stopped in to make sure I wasn't lying.

Maybe that was why he was helping.

84

He felt bad for assuming I was making it up.

Ha.

I knew *that* shit wasn't true.

Whatever his reasoning, he hung around until things slowed down, then followed me to my office. I peeled off my apron and headscarf, letting my locs fall free around my shoulders as he helped himself to my desk chair.

"Okay – you ready to explain what the hell you're doing here?" I asked, perching myself on the edge of the desk, facing him.

He shrugged, reclining back in my chair. "Just being a good Samaritan."

"Bullshit."

"Damn," he chuckled. "It's like that? That's what you think, that I'm not capable of being helpful out of the goodness of my heart?"

I raised an eyebrow. "I find it hella suspicious."

"Ms. Love, we work together, I'm subletting from your sister, you and I have been intimate, you're doing me the favor with my Aunt... I think we're at a place now where it shouldn't strike you as particularly odd that I'd come to your assistance when needed," Kadan reasoned.

"Still. Let's not forget all the shit that isn't so warm and fuzzy between us."

He scoffed. "Oh trust, I haven't. I still have nightmares about what that whole milk ice cream did to me."

"Yeah. Me too," I told him, shuddering over the thought. "Which is why I'm not sure I trust this whole *helpful* act."

A smirk spread over his lips. "Aiight real talk, Char said

you'd called about not being able to come in cause you were slammed. So I came to be obnoxious. I was bored, nothing better to do, so why not go be a pain in Jaclyn's ass?"

"Like a child with a crush who doesn't know how to act?"

He shrugged. "Possibly. But once I got here, and I saw that you were *for real* slammed... was I supposed to just sit back and watch?"

"You don't work here, so why not?"

"I... I don't know. Maybe it's a military thing. Sometimes, the shit that needed to be done wasn't my job, but the shit still needed to get done. So you get it done."

He was looking at me.

Not flirtatiously, not really, just *looking*.

Focused.

I cleared my throat, and looked away. "That's right," I nodded. "You were in the army. I bet you were like a *hoe* hoe. There's no way you weren't."

"Oh I was," he laughed. "Everybody is though."

"So the stereotype is true? Everybody fucking everybody?"

He nodded. "With a few, and I do mean *few* exceptions, hell yes."

"Figures," I giggled. "So tell me something... you're an army veteran, subletting an apartment, working at a community pet clinic. You're tattooed, you curse, you hoop with Jason. How the *hell* did Judge Calista Freeman end up with *you* as a nephew?"

Kadan tossed his head back, Adam's apple bobbing as he laughed. "I'm sure she asks herself that same question on a daily basis."

"So you don't code switch for Auntie?" I asked, and he shook his head.

"Not at all, and she can't stand it, but I am who I am, and

she's gonna love me anyway. Just like she is who she is, and I love her anyway. Even if I don't like her that much sometimes."

My eyebrows lifted. "Such as when?"

"Such as when she called me to complain about you," he teased, sitting up to scoot the chair closer. "Kadan Michael Davenport, do you know that woman has a *record*?! Fighting, vandalism, public intoxication, harassment, public nuisance, disturbing the peace, *more fighting!*"

I frowned. "She went through all my lil business, huh?"

"She didn't tell me *shit* I didn't already expect," Kadan laughed. "*But,* she was wrong for trying to put you out there like that, and I told her so. It wasn't cool."

"Wow, thank you for defending my honor, fake bae."

"I got you babe," he said, playfully grabbing me around the calf, and squeezing.

I was glad for my wardrobe choice of a cute spring wrap dress, even though my comfy Vans weren't the sexiest pairing with it.

My legs were freshly shaved though, at least.

"So is Judge Freeman your dad's sister, or your mom's?" I asked, shifting in my seated position on the desk.

"My mother's. My father – God rest his soul – was... let's say a rolling stone. You know, wherever—"

"He laid his hat was his home, I've got you," I nodded. "So your hoe-ness was inherited?"

"My mother and aunt like to think so," he good-naturedly agreed. "Aunt Cali couldn't stand him, but my mother loved his dirty draws, even though he wasn't good to her. Or *for* her. Sometimes I guess that's just the way shit goes though."

I sighed. "Yeah, unfortunately so."

"Unfortunate is the right word. I haven't seen her since his funeral. Barely talked to her either. Something about me reminding her too much of him or something. Some bullshit."

There was silence between us after he said that, while I tried to gauge the proper response. He wasn't giving the impression that this was a happy story by any means, but he also didn't seem particularly broken up about it.

Like he was numb to it.

"That's fucked up," was the response I settled on, and he nodded.

"Yeah. It is. Can't let the bullshit weigh you down though. What about you? You got mommy issues too?"

I shook my head. "Believe it or not... no. My parents are amazing, which I don't know... kinda makes me feel guilty?"

Kadan's brow wrinkled in confusion. "Why the *hell* would you feel bad about having great parents?"

"I don't feel bad about having great parents, I feel bad about my great parents having... me." My eyes went wide. "Wow, that sounds dramatic as fuck."

"It does," Kadan agreed. "I need you to explain that shit."

"Well, I can, because I've thought about it a lot. I think about it *all the time*," I admitted.

Why?

Who knows?

"It's like... my sisters, right? Jemma went to culinary school, travels the globe, knows foreign ambassadors and shit, never got in any trouble. Joia does her influencer thing, got her degree straightaway – again, never got in trouble. But then there's me. The fuckup. Constantly suspended in high school, had to do summer school, got kicked out of college the first go-round. I've had a record for the same length of time I've had a driver's license, but I'm not damaged. I'm not acting out. I'm not working through deep hidden trauma. I just am who I am, and that person is comfortable in handcuffs. Known on a first-name basis at the courthouse. It's *embarrassing*. Not for me though – for *them*."

Kadan stared at me for a moment, lips parted, then shook his head. "Nah, you're tripping," he said, brushing my words off. "I bet they don't even see it like that."

"Oh they definitely don't," I agreed. "But it doesn't change the fact that *I* see it. And the thing is, as much as I don't want to be *that* girl – don't want to ruin my life before I've even gotten started – *that* girl is just... who I am."

"Is it though?" Kadan scoffed.

I twisted my lips. "Man, you think I'm joking, but I'm dead ass serious. In high school – somebody messed with me, I was kicking ass. When I *left* high school, if somebody messed with me, I was kicking ass. *Now*, if somebody messes with me, I'm kicking ass. I ain't new to this, I'm true to this."

Kadan laughed. "I'm saying though – nobody can be mad about you defending yourself."

"That's not usually how the court sees it. Even if you weren't the one who started the shit, if you throw the first blow..."

"Well, *yeah*," Kadan chuckled. "I guess I'm trying to say that I get where you're coming from. Nobody wants to be messed with."

"And I got messed with *plenty*," I admitted. "*Flap Jacs*. That's what those little shitty ass kids used to call me, cause I was fat, right? I don't give a shit now, but back then, with my tall, slim, pretty older sisters? *Whooo*, it hurt like crazy. So I had to set a precedent. You fuck with *Flap Jacs*, oh we gone make pancakes, bitch, we gone smack, flip, and flatten," I said, laughing. "So shit, maybe I *was* dealing with some damage. But I never bothered anybody – I just wanted to be left alone. The rest of that stuff... got a little too drunk out with friends. Punched a dude in the face for calling one of my sister's out of her name. Ruined a motherfucker's car when I found out about his other family..."

"You've got hella stories, don't you?" he asked, and I nodded.

"Yep. I've had a colorful life, and now... I don't know. I'm just ready to settle into one specific palette. A *calm* palette."

"*Really?*" he asked, brows lifted. "I can't imagine that. At all. And not that it's up to me, but I can't understand why you want that?"

"You're right – it's *not* up to you."

I didn't want my private thoughts and desires challenged – I wanted him to shut up. And he did, but he didn't leave – he sat there staring at me, with this knowing smirk that made me want to squirm.

"What's so confusing about me wanting something different for my life?" I asked, letting curiosity get the best of me. "Why is not wanting to go to jail something to question?"

"That's not the questionable part," he answered immediately, like he'd just been waiting on me. "Limiting your colors. *That's* the part I don't get. That kaleidoscope is what makes you *Jaclyn*. It's what I was supposed to be keeping my ass away from."

"Wait a minute – *excuse me?*" I said, hooking my foot around the arm of the chair to roll him directly in front of me. "You're supposed to be keeping your ass away from me? Cause Auntie said so?"

He chuckled. "Nah, cause *I* said so."

"Why?"

"Because I have a definite type. Which hasn't been healthy for me in the past."

I planted my hands on either side of me on the desk, and leaned forward. "And what type is that?"

"Pretty ass thick women with bold personalities and attitude problems."

I narrowed my eyes, thinking about it for a second before I nodded. "That's an accurate description of me, I'll accept it. *After* you tell me about the big fine who hurt you and made you decide the rest of us were trouble."

"It wasn't like that," he laughed. "More like lack of self-control. Superior officers. Professors. Wives. Court reporters. Whatever. If I met her and I wanted her and she wanted me it was a done deal, consequences be damned. All the drama that came with it was part of the package."

"Ooooh. You weren't calculating trouble factors," I mused.

"I certainly wasn't. Got in some *shit* too. I've got fun memories and all, but that lifestyle of fucking whoever you want, whenever you want... some people can do that for the rest of their lives, but personally, I just want to be solid. No police at the door, no grade tampering, no threatening to put you on toilet duty, no suspicious cars following you home—"

"Oh, *damn*," I laughed. "You were like for real about the drama?!"

"Uh, *yeah*." He shook his head. "You have to remember, Jaclyn – I'm 34. I've been around longer than you. Time to get further around the block. Make mistakes of my own."

"Right, time to decide you wanted to be *solid*. But when I said I wanted to change *myyy* ways..."

He scoffed. "Nah, it's not the same thing though. You want

to be a better person, make better decisions, by all means, do that. But from the outside looking in, and admittedly not having known you long… I think you've already done the work with that shit. Before this thing with your ex, when was the last time you'd been in trouble?"

"Years. My Aunt – Jason's mom… when she died, she left money for all the kids. Like a *chunk* of money. Mine was in a trust, since I wasn't twenty-five yet, but my parents could access it for me. I'd already fucked over college the first time, and I had no idea what I was going to do with my life. So I traveled a bit, went to see Blackwood. There was a *Dreamery* there. The owner happened to be on site, so I spent time talking with her, and by the time I got back to *Blakewood*, plans were already in motion to open a fourth *Dreamery* location. This one."

Kadan smiled. "So you just bought an ice cream franchise?"

"Yep," I nodded, returning his smile. "My Aunt Priscilla was like a second mom, and I wanted to do something that would make her proud. I decided right then that the fighting and all that shit… it *had* to be over. I had to grow up. I wanted to be successful with my business, and finish school, and have a family. I wanted to be solid too. And then Victor happened."

I pushed out a deep sigh, dropping my gaze to the floral swirls of the fabric across my lap.

"As much as I hate to defend your actions that night," Kadan started, drawing my gaze to his face. "Since they *did* result in me having a black eye… you can't let that make you feel like you're going backward. Should you have fucked up his car? Of course not. But that was some heavy shit – you *lived* with that dude, and to find out what he had going on behind your back… shit, I would've snapped too. You had a moment, for sure, but that moment doesn't negate the years you spent rebuilding your life."

I scoffed. "Then why does it feel like it?"

"Because you have your past – something that embarrasses you – smacking you in the face right now. The car thing wasn't an isolated event because of your past, so your punishment for it was heightened. It's affecting you every single day. A constant reminder. And it's messed up, but it is what it is. But it's also why I feel like there's not shit for you to change, not in the immediate. You already did the changing, it's just this messed up situation has your mistakes under a spotlight right now. Your colors are fine though. Fuck a monochromatic."

That pulled a smile back to my face. "You're only saying that because I'm a 'pretty ass, thick woman, with a bold personality and an attitude problem.'"

"And I love that shit, so maybe you're right," he admitted, laughing. "But, I'm also a big proponent of being who the hell you are. Alcohol abuse and violence aren't personality traits – I had to learn that from experience myself. So yeah, that shit can be dropped, but everything else? People can embrace you, or they can move on."

"Listen to your "Kadan, Fix My Life" face ass," I giggled, then giggled louder when he grabbed my legs again, pulling them apart to roll between them.

"That your way of telling me you think I'm wise?" he asked, letting my feet rest in the space on either side of his hips, and propping his elbows on my knees.

Completely casual.

Like this was a thing we did.

Like this was our thing.

"With your face this close to my pussy, I'll call you anything you want me to call you," I said, hiking an eyebrow at him.

Those words made him smirk, and he lifted his hands to my thighs, pushing the fabric of my dress up. "Is that an invitation?"

"One where you might want to consider the fact that this cookie has been baking *all day* before you accept it."

His face balled in confusion for a second before understanding relaxed his features, and he laughed. Instead of backing off, he reached under my dress, hooking the side of my panties as he met my gaze. "Lift up."

I did.

Without a single second of hesitation.

With my hands gripping the lip of the desk, and my feet still planted in the chair with him, I pushed myself up, letting him slide my panties down over my hips.

"You just wear shit like this on a regular Tuesday, huh?" he asked, smirking as he pulled the pretty purple underwear down my legs and over my feet.

I shrugged, way more aware than usual of the rise and fall of my chest as he raised my feet, planting them on the arms of the chair before he rolled in ever closer.

"Pretty underwear makes me feel good."

Kadan pulled the brim of his hat around to the back of his head, then lowered his mouth to kiss the inside of my knee. "Nothing wrong with it. I was just asking."

"So," I breathed, gripping the edge of the desk even harder as those kisses drifted toward the insides of my thighs. "Can I *just ask* why you turned your hat around? You trying to look cool or something?"

He stopped what he was doing to hook my thighs over his arms, spreading me so wide that my dressed hiked all the way up to my hips, leaving me open and exposed. Kadan made this ultra-satisfied sound in his throat, then met my eyes with a grin.

"I want to know how you taste. I turned my hat around cause I don't need anything getting in the way."

I didn't have time to respond before his mouth was on me. *Holy.*

Shit.

My hands went immediately to his head, snatching the hat off so I could sink my fingers into the soft coils of his hair, holding his head in the right place.

Exactly the right place.

A deep shudder rushed from my lungs as his tongue lapped against me, sucking and pulling and prodding, coercing my body into producing fluids that were making it harder and harder to keep still on that desk.

"Oh *God*," I groaned, clenching my eyes tight as I tried my best to steady my ragged breathing. His fingers dug deep into the soft flesh of my thighs as he covered my clit with his mouth, torturing me with a delicious alternation between licking and sucking that made it hard to do anything except *feel*.

And *goddamn* did I feel good.

The rough, hot rasp of Kadan's skilled tongue was downright decadent, and I didn't bother trying to control myself from shamelessly rocking my hips into his face as he pressed deeper. My mouth fell open as exultations poured from my lips, and I'd never been more grateful for my employees' insistence on having the music in the shop up so loud.

It was drowning me out.

I *needed* drowning out, because Kadan's face between my legs was a *revelation*, and I wanted him to know it. After I came, with one hand gripping the desk, the other gripping a handful of his hair, he came up to do some necessary breathing of his own.

He grinned at me as he panted, his face and beard covered in the glistening evidence of what we'd just done. For a moment – *just* a teeny tiny moment – I understood why a woman might get on her knees and propose to a man.

I kiiinda wanted to lock that tongue down.

His gaze drifted up, to my head, and his smile grew even broader as he stood between my legs. "I like this energy," he declared, tugging down the brim of the hat – *his* hat – that I didn't even remotely recall placing on my head.

I couldn't formulate a response before he occupied my mouth with his. His tongue against my lips requested an invitation that I granted, greedily accepting him as he dipped into my mouth.

There was *nothing* timid about this kiss, this was the kiss of a man who knew exactly what he was doing, and exactly how I felt about what he was doing. How I felt was that he could do anything he wanted, including strip me out of my dress on top of my desk as if *Dreamery* weren't still open and conducting business hours.

As if I weren't supposed to be writing a paper.

My fingers were otherwise engaged though, with tugging off Kadan's shirt, then going for his sweats and boxers.

"Please tell me you have protection," I begged against his lips, breaking from kissing just long enough to make sure we could take this further than hunching.

I wasn't *above* hunching, and would hump this man to completion if I had to, but I *wanted* penetration.

Well.

At this point, *needed.*

"Wallet is in my pocket," he said, then resumed devouring my mouth while I dug the wallet out and fished out the condom.

Now I could do the big – *heh* – reveal on his dick, happy to see it was as perfect as it had been the other times I encountered it. I didn't waste any time getting it on him, and he didn't waste any time burying himself in me, then ridding me of my bra.

Never had I ever let a man strip me ass-naked in my office, let alone pull his dick out, but here we were, and I was *in love* with every second of it. That night at my house, I'd realized Kadan wasn't the type that just wanted to put his dick in you – he wanted to *consume* you, and I was willing to let him.

Give me all the slow strokes and hip action and long lusty looks, I silently urged as he stroked me like I was the girlfriend he'd claimed me to be – at least in front of his aunt. I hooked my legs around his waist, opening myself up more and simultaneously keeping him close as his hands cupped and squeezed my breasts, teased my nipples.

He dropped his mouth to my neck, sucking and biting as his hips moved to meet mine. My eyelids fluttered open, and I met someone's gaze.

My own.

Through the mirror on the wall.

I pushed out a relieved sigh that Kadan was too focused to even notice. He was too busy doing something with his tongue and teeth that felt amazing, but would undoubtedly leave a mark.

It was fine.

I took in my reflection – haphazard locs under his hat, glasses askew, glowing with sweat, mouth hanging open in pleasure while I got fucked in my office.

Completely unexpected.

And.... Totally fine.

Totally perfect, actually.

So of course someone knocked on the door.

"Go away!" I called, not even caring that I sounded like what was happening.

I *needed* the relief of the stress from today – hell, from the last few months-- and I had every intention of taking every piece of it.

Every stroke.

NINE

KADAN

"*WAKE UP, PUNK.*"

Okay.

So.

Maybe what *actually* came out of Miss Thing's mouth was "*meow*", but I'd spent enough time around animals to gauge what that shit really meant. Waking up to a cat on my chest – an *actual* cat, not the cutesy nickname of what I'd have gladly welcomed first thing in the morning – was a clear intimidation tactic, and I was no fool. So while Miss Thing still had her claws put away, I gently removed her to the floor, then pulled myself up.

Jaclyn wasn't in the bed.

It only took a quick peek into her main living space to find her though, passed out at her kitchen counter with her laptop still open. There was a message up on her screen that made me approach, peering at the words - a confirmation message that she'd properly submitted whatever the assignment had been. Presumably right before she passed out.

I couldn't help myself from grinning over how peaceful

she looked, glasses still on, full lips slightly parted, locs hanging halfway over her face. She was in just a tee shirt, most likely with nothing underneath, considering the circumstances behind me being here at all – a middle of the night text demanding I come through as her personal stress relief.

A text I'd eagerly answered because that was where I wanted to be anyway.

Fuck the games.

I was too old for it.

A quick glance at the time told me it was just past five in the morning – good timing for me to head back to my own place and get ready for the day before I headed to the clinic. From our conversation last night, I knew Jaclyn didn't have anywhere to be until a ten o'clock class. I didn't want to wake her.

But *I* had to leave, which meant it was necessary. I tried to do it as gently as I could, but she still popped awake like something was on fire, eyes wide as she took in her surroundings.

"What time is it?" she asked, groggy, as she straightened up, fixing her glasses on her face to check her computer.

"Like five-twenty," I told her. "You should go get in the bed."

"I need to check my answers first. I don't even remember submitting this." She stifled a yawn, then squinted at the computer.

I grabbed her hand. "You know that'll still be there after you get a couple more hours of sleep, right? You're obviously exhausted."

She shook her head. "I'm good, seriously," she insisted. "I have to check this, and then I have paperwork and stuff for

Dreamery that I have to do before class. And then I have a shift at the clinic this afternoon."

"Not today. Tonight is the ball... remember? Today is the first of your two weeks off."

"*Three* weeks off," she corrected, with a raised finger. "Don't play with me."

I grinned. "Just making sure you're actually awake. You *do* know what day it is, right?"

"It's Friday," she said, rolling her eyes. "I got my afternoons mixed up. I'm a busy woman, remember?"

"Yeah, I do, which is why I want you to understand – you don't *have* to do this. If you'd rather catch up on sleep, or work..."

She scoffed. "And deny the public a chance to see me in my fly ass dress? Are you crazy?"

"I'm just saying..."

"Uh-huh. *Just* keep that nonsense to yourself, and make sure you're here to pick me up on time. You *are* still picking me up, right?"

"Of course," I agreed. "For now though, I gotta throw my clothes on and get out of here so I can get to the clinic."

"Ah. So *that's* why you woke me up," she correctly deduced, and I nodded, moving back toward her room, where I'd left my clothes.

Despite her protests when I suggested it, Jaclyn followed me to the bedroom, climbing into the bed to snuggle under the covers and watch me get dressed.

"How did we end up here?" she asked, half-muffled by the pillow she'd partially buried her face in. "You've really got your pale ass in my apartment, wow."

"Why I gotta be pale?" I chuckled, pulling my boxers on. "I

got a lil melanin too, chill."

She laughed. "Yes, Kadan, you do, but your *actual* ass is hella pale."

"*Oh*. I don't think I've ever noticed."

"Why would you?" she asked, propping up on her elbow as I tugged my tee shirt over my head. "I only noticed because I was specifically looking... trying to figure out your appeal."

I stopped with my pants in hand, frowning. "Ain't shit to figure out shorty, I'm a handsome motherfucker and you know it."

"*Wow*," she laughed. "I wasn't suggesting otherwise, conceited much?"

"Nah, just a big fan of myself."

"I can *tell*," she assured me, in a dry tone. "You're an incredible example of Black male physicality, Kadan with the gold medal dick."

I grinned. "I'm ignoring your sarcasm cause your words are absolutely spot on. Thank you for noticing."

"Can you stop derailing my point?"

"You had one of those?"

I ducked the pillow she launched in my direction, then laughed as I pulled my pants back on.

"*Anyway*," she said. "I still want to know how the hell we got here, to DOD."

I raised an eyebrow. "DOD?" I asked, dropping into the chair in the corner to don my shoes.

"Dick-on-Demand. NetDicks. Dickazon Prime," she explained, with a distinct air of "*Duh*."

I shook my head. "Your mind..."

"Is amazing, I know," she said, beaming at me from her perch in the middle of the bed.

"That ain't the word I was looking for, but we'll go with that," I chuckled. "But to answer your question, in my humble opinion, we got here by being adults. We each have something the other wants, we admitted it, and now we both benefit. What's the problem?"

She shrugged. "I guess there isn't one. I guess."

"You guess?"

"It's not weird to you? That black eye I gave you was only like a month and a half ago. Yet, we've fucked several times, and I'm going to pretend to be your girlfriend at an alumni event tonight."

"And?"

"*And* we don't even really know each other," she argued. "What if somebody asks questions – how long we've been together, all that?"

"We tell the truth – well kinda. We met when I sublet your sister's apartment, kept running into each other, decided to see where it might go. That's barely a lie."

Hell it wasn't a lie at all.

But if I said *that*, she might freak out more than she was now.

"What if they ask *other* questions?"

"Anything more than that isn't their business, is it?"

She sighed, then flopped back into her remaining pillows. "I guess not, but still... it's hitting me right now how we've blurred these lines, and it's kinda fucking with me a little."

"What lines?" I asked. "I don't remember any lines."

Jaclyn sucked her teeth. "Dude, I distinctly asked you, before we messed around that first time, if you were gonna get attached."

"So that's what you think?" I looked up from lacing my

sneakers. "You think I've gotten attached?"

She sat up again, looking fine as hell with her locs all pushed to one side, wearing a smug grin. "Are you gonna tell me you haven't?"

"Are *you*?" I countered right back. "Cause I remember when you asked me that, I said I wouldn't if you didn't, and I'm *nothing* if not a man of my word."

"You can't even keep your word to yourself, Kadan! You told yourself to stay away from me, remember? And yet, here you are."

That smirk stayed on her face as I stood, walking up to the bed. "Yeah," I admitted. "Here I am." I leaned in, kissing her forehead. "But only because you asked for me, babe." I stepped back as the smugness melted from her face, and her eyes went wide.

I shot her a wink.

"See you tonight."

"**Y**ou look like you've got something heavy on the dome." I looked up from scrubbing my hands to find Kenzo in the doorway.

"Usual shit man," I told him as I grabbed paper towels to dry off. "You finished with the Harris family hamster?"

Kenzo cringed, shaking his head. "Man... the hamster finished with me, if you get my drift."

My eyes went wide. "Bruhhh. Unicorn Nuggets went on to glory?"

"It was a ten-year-old hamster – hell yeah it went on to glory. Did you see how that littlest one was handling him? I would've died too, if my folks were letting a three-year-old dress me in doll clothes for YouTube. Had that hamster in a halter dress and boots when they brought it in!"

I cackled. "You're a fool, man."

"I'm serious!"

"Stop *lying*," I shook my head, still laughing.

"I'm *not*. Look," he insisted, pulling out his phone. Sure enough, somehow the Harris' three-year-old daughter, Holly, had gotten the hamster into a zebra-striped halter dress and boots – one hot pink, one lime.

Unicorn Nuggets had experienced a hard life.

"Why did they let her do that to him?" I asked, handing the phone back. "I knew they called and said he was looking bad, but they didn't say *shit* about him coming in dressed like he was fresh off the corner."

Kenzo shrugged. "I don't know man, but the older daughter was steaming mad when I came out to let them know. Smacked her sister right in the head. Everybody screaming."

I shook my head. "I have never been so glad to be on neuter duty," I told him. "Better *you* have to deal with that bullshit than me."

"That's jacked up," Kenzo laughed. "But, speaking of bullshit, check this out – Char went out on a date."

I raised my eyebrows, waiting to hear the bullshit. When he didn't say anything else though, I frowned.

"What's wrong with that? She's attractive, smart, funny... why are you surprised?"

Kenzo groaned as he leaned against the shelf that housed the gloves and other sterilized gear. "I don't know... I guess I thought she would..."

"Wait on you?" I asked, and got a nice shock when his dumb

ass said-

"Yeah, a little."

"*No,*" I insisted. "*No. Naaah,*" I added, for emphasis. "That shit is over and done, these women aren't hanging around waiting on your ass to figure out if you want them anymore. I *told* you to go ahead and make that move, don't be salty now."

"Nah, I'm high-sodium as hell right now," Kenzo countered. "I was just waiting on the perfect time. This feels like a betrayal."

"You've gotta be kidding me," a female voice sounded, and both of our eyes went wide as Char stepped in through the open door, arms crossed. Her eyes were full of fire, but lucky for me, she pointed that anger straight at Kenzo.

I took a couple of steps back, and subtly pulled my phone out.

"You weren't waiting for the perfect time, Kenzo, you were putting me on hold. Cause you thought I'd wait while you played around, but guess what – *I won't.*"

"I wasn't *playing,*" Ken argued. "Seriously, I just... I didn't want to take it there until I was sure."

"So you expected me to sit around and twiddle my thumbs? I've done everything short of directly handing you my panties, and you *always* play it off. So, yeah, I'm going to date. A lot. And I'm going to stop thinking about *you.*"

Kenzo grabbed Char by the arm as she turned to leave, stopping her. "Hold up – you're saying I don't even have a *chance* now?"

"Why should you?"

"Because of this."

Hell, *my* eyes went wide when he grabbed her by the face to kiss her – and not a peck, either. Homeboy went *all the way* in, and I was trapped in the corner, afraid to interrupt their moment.

When they pulled away from each other, Char squared her shoulders, and cleared her throat.

"Fine," she told him. "One date. And you'd *better* make it count."

With that, she walked off, with Ken right behind her, neither of them looking back to where I was. Grinning, I shook my head and stopped the video, sending it to Jaclyn along with the words, ***"Your influence."***

For as long as I'd known Char, I'd *never* known her to be bold like that.

Jaclyn had been in her ear.

I was still chuckling about that whole thing by the time I made it back to my office to go through my paperwork for the day. I'd spent the whole morning preventing unwanted reproduction, and now I had to do the other part, so that we weren't putting too much on Char. Since I was taking away her help for three weeks due to my deal with Jaclyn, it was only right that I took as much as I could off her plate.

"You didn't have to be so quick to tell on me, you know."

An immediate grin came to my face as Char stepped into the office, arms crossed.

"I'm guessing that means Jaclyn hit you up," I said, and she nodded. "I wasn't telling on you though – I was bragging. Proud of you for putting Kenzo's ass on the spot."

Char couldn't help the smile that spread over her face as she stepped in and closed the door – probably so *we* couldn't be snooped on the way she had on my conversation with Ken.

"I've known you a long time, Kadan... we're friends, right?"

I raised an eyebrow. "As far as I know, yeah... why?"

"I want you to tell me the truth about Ken."

"The truth? I'm not su—*oh*. You want to know what his trouble factor is like."

Char frowned. "Trouble factor?"

I've been around Jaclyn way too much…

"Whether or not he's gonna mess around. Break your heart."

"Oh. *Yes.*"

I nodded, sitting back in my desk chair. "Char, I can't give you a definite answer one way or another on something like that – I don't have that kind of knowledge. But I know Ken to be a stand-up guy, and I believe that he cares for you a lot – enough that he was hesitant to involve himself with you, for fear of hurting you."

"Isn't that a *bad* sign though?"

I shook my head. "Nah. What's concerning is when a man *isn't* concerned that he might mess up."

"I guess that's true," Char nodded. "I just… I don't want it to be awkward around here, if it doesn't work out. I love my job, and I don't want anything to mess that up."

I scoffed. "Y'all already swapped spit though, so…"

"*Kadan.*"

"What?" I laughed. "I'm just saying… if it doesn't work out, and it *is* awkward, it'll pass, and we'll be a family again. If I can get past the awkwardness of working with Ms. Love after she socked me in the eye, I feel like we can all get past most things."

Char smirked. "There's a good chance sleeping together makes getting through the awkwardness a much smoother transition."

My eyes went wide. "She told you we were sleeping together?"

"She didn't have to – it's *so* obvious when y'all are in a room together, and why else would you be giving her time off from volunteering?"

"The kindness of my heart?"

"Oh *please*." Char rolled her eyes. "I kinda knew it was coming from the night she walked in with that cat. Your whole demeanor changed."

"She had a cat in a bowl of chicken," I defended – a defense that made her laugh.

"Sure, you can say it was that, or you can admit that you were interested. And you can admit that you're full-blown smitten now."

I couldn't deny that.

So I didn't try.

"Fine. Maybe I am. Jaclyn is intelligent, fine as hell, successful, vivacious, funny... she's an easy woman to admire."

Char smiled as she walked back to the door, pulling it open. "I agree."

"You agree with what?" Kenzo asked, wearing a goofy ass grin as he approached the open doorway.

"That Jaclyn is a great match for him."

"Oh absolutely," Ken agreed, nodding. "Shouldn't you be heading out soon to get ready – I thought you were taking her to that alumni ball thing tonight, that's why you wanted the early shift today?"

"Yes." I sat up, propping my elbows on my desk as Char turned with wide eyes. "I was wrapping up some work before I left."

"You got a tux for this, right?" Char asked. "And a limo?"

I frowned. "Uh... nah. I got the Charger detailed though."

Kenzo chuckled as Char's mouth dropped open. "You're taking her to a *ball* in a *Charger*?"

"What, it's a nice ass car!" I called to Char's retreating back as she walked off, mumbling about my *typical army fuckboy vehicle* choice.

She wasn't wrong, but still.

It *was* a nice ass car.

And it *was* freshly detailed.

"You feel me, don't you Ken?" I asked, and he held up his hands.

"I *just* got in good with her – you're on your own, man. But good luck tonight."

He walked off too, leaving me wondering what the hell the problem was – not that I had much time to think about it. I had plenty to do, including a fresh haircut and getting my tux from the cleaners', as well as a stop at the flower shop.

I was going to make the best I could out of this night.

"*Gaaahdamn*." was my immediate reaction when Jaclyn opened the door.

Really, it was the only appropriate response to seeing her in a sleeveless dress that fit like a glove from her breasts down to her hips, then flared into a full skirt down to the floor. Her locs were pinned up in an intricate style, her perfect lips painted deep red. She'd even switched glasses, from her usual trendy black ones to a frameless style that allowed you to see more of her gorgeous face.

"*Kadan stop it!*" she half-screamed, half-giggled, as I swept her up into my arms and kicked her door closed behind us. "You're gonna mess up my makeup," she whined – then moaned – as my lips met her collarbone.

"I guess you'll just have to do it again," I growled into her neck as I carried her into the bedroom, dropping her onto the bed before I pounced on top of her.

"Kadan, *wait.*"

"*Whooooo!*"

"*Right in front of my salad?*"

"*Took forty-minutes to connect this call, they aint even gone make it to that ball.*"

"*Bow-chicka-wow-wow!*"

"*He's got a nice wide back, don't he?*"

"*Josephine, stop looking at that boy! Boy get your ass off my daughter!*"

I went tense for a second before I scrambled off of Jaclyn, looking around for the source of the other voices in the room.

"*Oh my God,*" Jaclyn grumbled as she sat up. "Kadan... meet my *entire* family."

She lifted a finger, and my gaze followed where she was pointing to land on her laptop, where she was apparently connected to a video call with several other people. I recognized Jemma, and assumed the other young woman must be their middle sister, Joia. In a different screen was an older couple – a scowling man I assumed was her father, and a smiling woman who looked too much like Jaclyn to not be her mother.

"*Hiiii Kadan!*" the women chimed, and I scrubbed a hand over the freshly faded side of my head.

"Uh... hey ladies," I greeted, with a little wave.

"Okay, that's enough of this," Jaclyn insisted, rushing toward the laptop. "You've seen the dress and everything, which cost me near an hour, and now, I gotta go."

"*Don't forget the toweeelllll,*" one of her sisters called out as Jaclyn slammed the top closed on the laptop.

"Well. That was *lovely*," Jaclyn said, pulling in then pushing out a deep breath through her nose.

"My bad," I told her, stepping closer so I could grab her hand. "You just look so good, I couldn't help myself."

"I *do* look good, don't I?"

"Beyond." I leaned down to press a kiss just below her ear, respecting her wish to not have her makeup disturbed. "Let's go ahead and get out of here – sooner we show our faces, the sooner we can leave and I can mess this up without you getting mad at me. Deal?"

She smiled. "Deal. The car is waiting downstairs?"

"Um... *my* car is waiting downstairs."

That beautiful smile melted off her face.

"Nigga. I *know* you aren't taking me to the ball in that Charger."

Um.

Okay.

Maybe I should've thought it through a little more.

Because I didn't, I didn't have any choice other than to take the good-natured roasting that filled the whole trip there in stride. It had us both in a great mood by the time we arrived on campus and pulled up to the valet, joining the line of BSU graduates young and old and in-between as everyone filtered into the event space.

For a good minute, we were having a nice time – Jaclyn and I both ran into professors we'd had and enjoyed, along with some classmates. It was fun catching up with everybody, and my mood was shifting from "get this shit over with" to "damn, I'm glad we came".

And then, Aunt Cali walked up, with Deidre on her arm.

Visually, I could never, *ever* front on Deidre – she was fine as hell. It was too bad that fineness came with the wrong kind of drama.

"Kadan, I see you made it," Aunt Cali greeted me, with a smile and her standard kiss on the cheek. Her gaze flitted to Jaclyn, long enough for her displeasure to be clear before she smiled again, and turned to Deidre. "Of course you remember the lovely DeeDee," she said, prompting Deidre to pull me into a hug that was too tight and lingered too long – I practically had to pry her ass off me.

"Of course," I agreed, frowning as I straightened my jacket. "And I know *you* remember *Jaclyn*," I said, putting an arm around her waist to pull her into my side. "My beautiful date."

Aunt Cali hiked her chin. "Right. I scarcely recognized you outside the courtroom, dear."

"*Oh*," Deidre exclaimed, in that fake-ass chipper voice of hers that grated my nerves. She reserved it for public use. "Is *this* the delinquent you told me about?"

Beside me, Jaclyn stiffened. "*Bitch*. I'm only letting Judge Freeman's fermented ass slide because I don't want to give her a stroke, but *you...*"

I squeezed her, bending to whisper for only her to hear, "*Chill, please.*"

She blew out a sigh. "You just be glad I'm committed to not catching another charge."

"How horribly *rude*," Aunt Cali declared, as if she wasn't the one who started the shit – a fact I was about to bring up when she grabbed Deidre to walk away. "I see someone I need to speak to." She had to have known I wasn't about to let that shit go, from the way she rushed off with Deidre in tow.

"I'm sorry about that," I told Jac, shaking my head as they left.

She shrugged. "Not your fault she's an asshole. I just want her to stay the hell away from me. The Wrights are over there though," Jac added, pointing in the direction opposite of where my Aunt and Deidre had gone. "Let's go say hi."

We did more than say hi.

We ended up spending the next half hour posted up with them, and I was glad for it. That run-in could have ruined the night, but the Wrights were Jaclyn's family. If she couldn't be comfortable around anybody else, she could be comfortable around them.

Unfortunately, we couldn't keep them to ourselves.

Most of the Wrights were considered distinguished Blakewood alums themselves, so there were others in the room who wanted face time with them. It wasn't until we were away from that bubble of familiarity that we both realized the same messed up thing.

"Kadan am I imagining shit, or does it seem like there's a lot of people looking at me?"

She *wasn't* imagining it.

All it took was a glance to where my Aunt Calista and Deidre were standing off to the side wearing smug grins and sipping champagne to confirm it.

"*Hell nah,*" I heard Jaclyn mumble, and before I could stop her, she was off, walking right up to where they were standing. "What the *hell* is your problem?" she demanded, just as I joined her side.

"Do you see?" Aunt Cali asked, addressing me as if Jac wasn't even there. "All these important people around, and yet she has no problem *attempting* to make a scene."

Beside her, Deidre huffed. "You can bring a ratchet to culture, but you can't make her think."

"Oh I *think* plenty, *bitch. Thinking* about it is the only thing keeping me off your ass right now," Jaclyn snapped, as I hooked her again, hoping that if she *did* decide to swing on Deidre, I could intervene.

"She doesn't belong here," Aunt Cali sang, pulling an even deeper frown to my face.

"Auntie, cut the bullshit, okay?" I responded, at the same time Jaclyn spoke up for herself too.

"I belong here as much as anybody else – I'm a Blakewood student too, soon to be alumni, *and* I own a successful business in this community. My sisters went here, my parents went here, my cousins went here. My *ancestors* went here, maybe even further back than you, and I bet they would be completely disgusted with you treating people like you're better than they are."

"We just call like we see it," Deidre sneered.

"Man shut your ass up," I snapped, hauling Jaclyn backward when I felt her pulling against my hold around her waist. "You're always up my Auntie's ass trying to be her clone – take a breather."

Deidre reeled back like I'd smacked her, but my concern for Jac weighed a helluva lot more than that girl's hurt feelings.

"Hey," I said, keeping my voice low for just her, since a bit of a crowd had gathered. "Seriously, you gotta chill."

Jaclyn's eyes were already glossy, but they narrowed at my words, and she shoved out of my hold. "Right. Let me go do that. I need to use the restroom," she declared, holding her head high as she moved off in the opposite direction.

As soon as she was gone, I turned right to my Aunt Calista, who was comforting Deidre as if their asses weren't the ones in the wrong.

"What the *fuck* is wrong with y'all?" I asked, not giving a damn who overheard me.

Aunt Cali's eyes went wide as hell, traveling around the crowd before they came back to me, full of anger. "How *dare* you speak to me this way, and in front of people?!"

"How dare you speak to *her* that way?" I growled right back. "You can dish bullshit, but you can't take it?"

"You will *respect* me, young man!"

"You don't know shit about respect," I countered. "If you did, you wouldn't have pulled whatever you pulled that had people looking upside Jaclyn's head like she was about to draw a weapon."

Aunt Cali huffed. "Are we *that* certain she won't?!"

"You know that's bullshit. You *know* that's bullshit," I repeated, shaking my head. "And I would think you, of all people, would understand giving a young woman a chance to grow from her mistakes, but I see you're selective with your memory."

"I have no idea what you're talking about."

My face screwed into a scowl. "I'm talking about your *sister*. *Carmen*. My *mother*! Remember her?!" I asked. "The drug dealing, the prostitution, my father having to take custody? You managed to clean her up, get her record cleared, and now you don't remember none of that, huh?"

"This is *not* the place—"

"You *made it the place*," I interrupted. "What, you scared for all your lil' bougie fake friends to know you had crime in your own family? That you threw your power around so—"

Aunt Cali stepped toward me, nostrils flared. "Kadan Michael Davenport, that is *enough*," she hissed.

I laughed at that shit though. "Is it?! You're embarrassed?

You shamed, Auntie? But you didn't have any issue putting Jaclyn's business out in front of these people. No problem making *her* feel bad, huh?"

"*She is not good enough for you.*"

"Because she messed up in the past? So we gonna act like you didn't pull strings for me to go to the military instead of my rightful punishment for that drunk and disorderly and assault charge?"

"*Kadan...*" She was for real pleading with me now, and even Deidre was looking at her sideways, cause that was something she didn't know – something *nobody* knew, because my Aunt had done a good ass job of burying it, just like the shit with my mother.

Burying the shit didn't undo it though.

"Just... *stop.*" I shrugged. "Just stop it, aiight? I *love you* Aunt Cali, but this is not okay, and it won't ever be okay. I like Jaclyn, full stop, and I don't give a shit what you think about her, because I am a grown ass man. I was trying to preserve your feelings, trying to put a little sugar on this, but I see that was a mistake, so let me say it like this – stay outta my personal life. I've got it."

I didn't wait for her to respond before I turned away, scanning the crowd for Jaclyn. When I didn't see her, I headed to where I knew the bathrooms were, and waited. After several minutes passed, I stopped someone coming out to ask about her, but they swore she wasn't in there – even went back in to check for me. That led me outside, thinking she'd gone to get some air, but even then, I couldn't find her.

"You looking for somebody?" the dude at the valet stand asked. Recognizing him from when we first arrived, I nodded.

"Yeah, you remember the woman I came in with?"

A smirk spread over his face. "Mmmhmmm, I sure do. That woman was *fine*."

"Yeah, I know – have you seen her?"

"Mmmhmmm, I sure have."

"Okay, *where*," I prompted, when he didn't immediately answer.

"She ordered a ride on the cell phone," he told me, shaking his head. "Looked *real* upset. I'm telling you, you better take care of a woman that looks like that, or somebody else will."

"Thank you," was my dry response, and I slipped him a few bills from my pocket too.

Fuck.

I raked a hand through my thick hair, thinking back through the night to figure out what *I* had done to piss her off enough for her to leave without saying anything.

Hell.

Maybe that didn't even matter. She was only here to pretend for me anyway, so maybe she'd had her fill with the bullshit with my Aunt.

I was ready to dip too, so I couldn't even blame her.

I pulled out my phone to see if she'd sent a text, but there was nothing there from her. I shot her one of my own, asking her to let me know once she'd made it home safely before I went back to the valet to request my car.

Briefly, I thought about stopping by her place, but after the shit with my Aunt... she probably needed space to breathe. Reluctantly, I set my course for my apartment, hoping to get a text back from her by the time I made it there.

If not... space be damned.

I'd see her tomorrow.

TEN

JACLYN

"Why are men?"

I posed that question to my sisters and then took another long drink of wine, straight from the bottle.

"Why are men... what, Jac?" Jemma asked. She was coming in from a night out herself, and I'd caught Joia up doing her meal prep for the following week.

"Yeah," Joia chimed. "Your drunk ass didn't finish the question."

"I'm not drunk, and I *did* finish the question. *Why are men?* Dassit. That's the question. Just why at all?"

Jemma sighed. "Girl, why *indeed*. Remember the guy I was telling you about from the other day?"

"The 'transcendent' dick you told us about in vivid detail?" Joia giggled. "How could we possibly forget? Actually - never mind, I did forget. Tell it again."

"Well, I would if I wasn't feeling some kinda way about his ass dropping off the map without bothering to say goodbye! I woke up and his ass was gone. And I'm in Havana, so it's not like I might even run into him again. He's not from here either."

Joia sucked her teeth. "Sounds like a perfect affair. Assuming of course that he didn't take - or leave anything you can't get rid of - when he went."

"Oh that's not an issue. Can't be a hoe in every international country code without precautions."

"Don't tell me you caught feelings for this one?" I interjected.

"For him? No. For his sex?... Maybe."

That set off a round of laughter between the three of us, because we'd all been there.

Unfortunately.

"Well, at least you've got good memories from your latest *'Why are men?'* encounter," Joia spoke up. "I, on the other hand, have Theodore Graham in my inbox talking about a collab. Nigga, collab my cheeks and kiss. Ugh!"

Under my breath, I snickered, and from the silence on the phone line, I had every reason to suspect that Jemma was doing the same. Teddy was one of Joia's peers in the small circle of popular social media influencers in the growing Blakewood population. While Joia was more focused on women's health, beauty, fitness, and the like, Teddy was all about laughs, haircuts and sneakers, with sports commentary thrown in.

Oh, and he was Joia's first love.

And first heartbreak.

She couldn't stand his ass.

"It ain't funny!" Joia declared, correctly surmising that we were laughing. "He gets on my nerves."

Jemma chuckled. "I think you're still holding on to residual feelings for Teddy Grahams."

"Tuh. The cereal *only*. Which he ruined for me, by the way!"

I scoffed. "Oh please, Miss Fit Bitch," I laughed. "Your ass wouldn't be caught dead with a box of cereal anyway."

"Don't be making sense in my face Jaclyn!" she countered, struggling to keep herself from laughing too, cause she knew it was true. "Speaking of fitness, you should bring your ass back to the gym with me. There's a new boxing instructor," she sang.

"You mean, to replace the one Jaclyn ran off?" Jemma asked.

"*He told me to give it everything I had!*" I defended myself. "Not my fault he got his ass kicked. And Joia was the one who vlogged it."

"My bad."

We all broke into laughter about *that* shit too.

"Okay sis," Jemma spoke. "You've told us all about Kadan's bitch Aunt, and raggedy Deidre, who I think I might know, but that's a different conversation. When are you going to tell us what *Kadan* did?"

Joia scoffed. "Not until she figures that part out herself."

"Oh shut up," I said, even though she was right. I knew how I felt, I just hadn't yet figured out how to verbalize aloud to explain to my sisters.

I just wished he'd been different.

Not that he *owed* me different, when the only reason I was even at the ball with him was to make excuses for his aunt. A woman who had no issue telling me to my face that she didn't think I was good enough for Kadan.

Which... no lie, those words hit different in the face of the fact that he and I were sleeping together... nothing more.

Hell, maybe *Kadan* didn't think I was good enough for him – all that *"calm down"* energy he had for *me* while those other bitches were the ones creating the problem...

I shouldn't have been surprised.

"Jac, listen – fuck them, if they can't see how *incredibly* dope you are, okay?" Joia said. "A hater bitch ain't *never* stopped the *Love* story, and we're not about to let it now. You're fine as hell, you own a business, and you'll officially have a degree in a few weeks. You *are* still doing that, right?"

I sucked my teeth. "Don't even play with me. My graduation application was in by the deadline, my regalia is ordered, my advisor is on board, approved everything... I'm definitely walking across the stage, but whether or not I actually *get* the degree... that relies on me not dropping the ball right here at the end."

"Which has to be a difficult balance," Jemma mused. "You have a *lot* going on. Especially with the addition of this community service mess."

"Yeah," I huffed. "I was busy enough without it, and now... I've barely felt like I had time to breathe."

"But it'll be over soon. You basically just have finals, right?"

"Yes. Papers on papers. All the papers. Details this week," I said, closing my eyes. I didn't want to think about that.

"Well, we're here if you need us, Jac, you know that," Joia said.

Jemma agreed. "Whatever you need us to do."

"Just have your asses in the stands to watch me come across that stage."

That wasn't in question anyway, and they made sure I knew that before we got off the phone. I knocked back the rest of my wine and tossed my cell onto my bedside table, fully ready to pass out asleep until I heard the distinct rapping of a fist at my front door.

It was *way* too late for unannounced visitors, but tipsy curiosity wouldn't allow me to simply ignore it. I fought my way out of bed and trudged to the door, rolling my eyes when I saw who was on the other side of the peephole.

"What do you want?" I called through the closed door.

"To make sure you're okay – you're not answering your phone, or replying to texts," Kadan answered. The sound of his voice – even muffled – cut right through my annoyance with him to latch onto the natural horniness that plagued me every time I drank.

Shit.

"That's because I blocked your number!"

"*Blocked?*" Kadan called back, confused. "What the hell did I do?"

Before I could stop myself, or had any sort of plan, I'd unlocked the door and snatched it open. "*Nothing.* That's what! While those two bitches humiliated me, all your puppy-healing ass did was tell *me* to chill!"

He frowned. "I was trying to *help* you," he argued. "You're the one who was talking about wanting to change – not fighting and shit anymore, which is what they were trying to goad you into. So you'd get in trouble again, which is what you didn't want."

"Why didn't you tell *them* to chill?"

His hands went up. "I could've sworn I did, multiple times, before you walked off, and I *definitely* got in their asses about it after, but Jac... they weren't my concern at the moment. *You* were. I wanted to make sure *you* were good. But obviously I fucked that up, so tell me what you'd like me to do next time something like that happens."

I blinked. "Next time?"

"Yes. Not that we'd *want* something like that to happen

again, but shit... just in case. Tell me how to make sure you feel taken care of."

For several seconds I stared at him, lips parted, trying to make sense of what the hell was happening, but... shit, I couldn't. I shook my head. "I can't deal with this right now."

I turned to walk away from the door like this wasn't *my* apartment, and Kadan followed me inside, closing it behind him.

"Can't deal with what right now?" he asked, so... *God*, so endearingly confused that it pissed me off – and turned me on – at the same damn time. "And why are you still in your dress?"

Shit.

Because my tipsy ass can't undo the hook wasn't an answer I was about to give him, not in this state, so I focused on the other, more loaded, question.

"I cannot deal with you coming in here with this... I don't know, concerned boyfriend act. This whole little stupid fake bae shit is over, Kadan – and was a massive fail by the way. Judge Freeman is *never* going to let you rest. She's not going to let *me* rest either. So thanks for that."

That goofy bewilderment melted from Kadan's face, replacing itself with frustrated resolve. "My Aunt isn't going to do shit to you – trust me on that. She knows she took this shit too far, and I've got the voicemail theatrics to prove it."

"Is that supposed to make me feel better?"

He shook his head. "*Better*? No, probably not. But her fucking with you can be one less concern on your mind."

"Noted," I shrugged. "Now what?"

"Now," he started, stalking toward me so fast that my brain had barely registered his approach before he was behind me, unhooking my dress, which had started to painfully dig into my flesh. "We talk about this *'whole lil stupid fake bae shit.'* He smirked as he stepped back around in front of me, even though there was only a little space between me and the couch. "And I point out that I *never* called you that, and the only time I faked a thing was the day I asked you to do it."

I narrowed my eyes. "Okay, and what is that supposed to mean?"

"What do you mean, *what does it mean?* It *means* I'm not faking this shit, Jaclyn."

"Okay, and what is *that* supposed to mean?"

Kadan chuckled as he perched on the arm of the couch, pulling me between his legs. "It means that every time I've called you babe, every time I've kissed you, every time I've sought you out, or came sprinting because you summoned me... it's only been because I *wanted* to, not to put on a show."

I blinked, hard.

"Okay and what is that supposed to *mean?*"

Again, he laughed. "It means at some point, without either of us realizing it, I decided you were mine, for real. And I have every intention of acting accordingly." He reached up, cupping my face in his hand to draw me closer. Our lips were almost touching when he tensed, and pulled back. "Wait you *blocked* me?"

"Hm?"

"Seriously?"

The exasperated expression on his face instantly put me on defense.

"Yeah, *seriously,*" I said, propping a hand on my hip. "As far as *I* could tell, it seemed like you were more on their side than mine, and I thought you thought you were too good for me. Or something."

He blew out a sigh. "What have I ever done to make you think I thought you weren't good enough for me?"

"Well we can start with the criminal record jokes," I snapped.

"And we can end with those too, because it was that – *jokes*. Do you seriously think I'm judging you *for real* about that shit? Jac, if it wasn't for me knowing somebody who knows somebody, *I'd* have a record too."

My eyebrows shot up. "I didn't know."

"No, you didn't. But the more important point is, I know it's a sensitive topic for you now, so I won't make those jokes. Because we communicated about it. You talked, and explained an issue, giving me a chance to rectify that issue before you *blocked* me."

"Why do you keep *saying that*?!"

He scoffed. "Why did you *do* it?!"

"Because you hurt my feelings!"

"With *jokes*? Jaclyn, you have roasted me about pretty much every facet of my life, and you can't take *jokes*?"

I crossed my arms. "You know what? Fuck this, if you're going to be mean," I said, turning to walk away.

Kadan didn't let me get far, grabbing my elbow to bring me right back between his legs. "Bring your ass back here, ain't nobody being mean to you. We're *gonna* talk about this shit, and get past it, because this is... this is *nothing*, aiight? I am sorry, truly, for making you feel unworthy, because it's the furthest thing from what I believe. From the moment I met you, I *knew* you were somebody I'd get wrapped up in, and here we are."

"Which is *where*, Kadan?"

"With me sitting in front of you putting all my shit on the line right now, *Jaclyn*," he countered. "I *want you*, and I don't know how to be any more transparent about it. I *like you*. I like your energy, I like your sense of humor, I like your brain, I like your face, I like your booty," he said, grabbing it for emphasis and making me laugh. "I like you," he repeated. "And I'm aged out of playing games when it comes to that. So yeah, that's where we are. We're at *Jaclyn has to make a decision*."

I blew out a sigh, and shook my head. "What if I can't make a decision? What am I supposed to do with *any* of this? I got my heart *shattered* like six weeks ago, or something, and I haven't even begun to process it because I haven't *had time*. Because I have too much to do to grieve a relationship. Can you even imagine? I haven't let myself think about it, because I don't have time to be a mess behind a breakup. I had to find a new place, and take care of a cat, and keep up my grades, and run a business, and repay my debt to society, and *now* you want me to make a decision because *you like me*. Well guess what, Dr. Doolittle - *I don't have the bandwidth!*"

I tried my best to snatch away, but he wouldn't let me – instead, he stood, wrapping his arms tight around my shoulders. That was all it took for the tears to come, and I couldn't do anything but melt into his hold, accepting the comfort he was offering.

Comfort I was grateful he was willing to give, because *seriously Jac?! WHAT THE FUCK?*

I had no idea where any of that had come from. Which I guess was a sign my subconscious suppression of everything Victor related had worked beautifully. I *hadn't* given myself any time to process that breakup, and now here I was a short time later with a different man – a *better* man – wanting me.

Wanting more than I could fathom having to give right now.

"I'm sorry," he muttered into my hair, kissing the top of my head. "You're right. I didn't realize."

I shook my head, peeling myself back enough to look up and meet his gaze. "It's not your fault. You just happened to be here when it all came out."

He raised his hands to my face, using his thumbs to wipe the moisture from my cheeks. "Doesn't mean I can't be sorry for adding to the stress of it all."

"You've actually been a good stress relief these last few weeks. I appreciate it."

"Glad I could be of service to you." He pushed out a sigh, and took a step back from me. "I think it would be good if we *didn't* do that though."

"... what?"

"I'm saying, maybe we shouldn't see each other for a bit? You know? Give you time to finish school, get yourself settled. And we won't see you at the clinic until *after* you graduate."

My chest tightened, and fresh tears pricked at my eyes. "You're mad at me."

"*No*," he answered, shaking his head. "No, Jaclyn. Not at all."

"Then why are you doing this? Why are you saying this?"

"You think I *want* this?"

I shrugged. "Maybe so! If it's not what you want, why would you do it?"

"Because it's what *you* need," he countered. "What I heard from you is that you're stressed and overstimulated with everything t going on. That you need peace. That you need *time*. So that's what I'm trying to give you!"

"Okay so why can't we do what we've *been* doing?" I asked, trying not to sound as desperate as I felt.

Kadan shook his head, giving me a smile. "Because I want more than what we've been doing. If you don't, that's fine, we can go on about our lives. But if you're telling me you need time and space to make a decision, then let's do that. Let's do it the right way."

"This doesn't feel like the right way," I admitted. "It doesn't feel good, at all."

"It rarely does."

Finally, he approached me again, taking my face in his hands. This time he didn't pull back, instead granting me a kiss filled with a sweet sort of intensity I could hardly handle without bursting into tears again.

"Stop acting like I'm breaking up with you," he whispered against my lips. "I'm giving you a break from *me*."

"Shut up," I whispered back. "You're not making it better."

"Sorry." He kissed my forehead, and let me go. "It's a few weeks. A few weeks, and then we'll see what happens."

I knew what was going to happen.

He was going to walk out of here, and we'd never find our way back to the moment of possibility, where there might have been something between us. I wanted to take it all back, wanted to not have drunk that whole bottle of wine, wanted to not have left the ball alone, whatever it would have taken for this night to not have ended this way.

But I couldn't take it back.

I'd told my truth, and he'd told his, and I *couldn't* take any of it back, even though this shit hurt.

It hurt bad, actually, because I...

Shit.

I liked him too

A lot.

But I would be lying if I took back anything I said, and even though I knew what it meant... I had to let him walk out my front door.

a few weeks later -

"*Jaclyn Love.*"

Whew.

I'd never, *ever* been so glad to hear my name called.

Not, *Jaclyn Love, you're under arrest*, or *Jaclyn Love, you're sentenced to*, or *Jaclyn Love, get your ass...* none of that. Just my name, paired together with the degree I'd earned, spoken aloud.

I promised myself I wouldn't cry about it, but I broke that promise as soon as I heard the seemingly thunderous reaction of my family as BSU's president placed the symbolic diploma in my hand, and moved my tassel from one side to the other. I couldn't help myself – I burst into tears, because this shit had been a long time coming, and had taken *so* much out of me.

But I'd made it.

My huge family group descended on me as soon as the ceremony was over, making me smile for what felt like hundreds of pictures, but I didn't mind, at all. It was amazing to have them all there for me – my parents, Joia, Jemma and the Wrights too – Jason, Reese, Justin, Toni, Joseph, Devyn, Imara and my Uncle Joe, and all the kids. Even Kenzo showed up, with Char on his arm, and several of my people from *Dreamery*.

Everybody.

It felt really, *really* good.

With the exception of this one face I hoped to see, but obviously... didn't.

I shouldn't have been surprised – with Kenzo and Char at

the ceremony, *somebody* had to be there for the animals of Blakewood, but I couldn't pretend it didn't sting. I was careful not to bring him up – not to Kenzo or Char, or to Jason – and they didn't bring him up either.

I *wanted* to ask though.

Badly.

But I refused to be pressed about him if he wasn't pressed about me.

He sent flowers though, remember?

Yeah.

Okay, fine.

So, he sent the most gorgeous, huge bouquet of congratulatory roses the day before the graduation ceremony, along with a small lemongrass plant for Miss Thing. I *had* been happy about it, and fully expected to see him there with everybody else to celebrate.

The wrong expectation, apparently.

This was a happy day though, my celebration. So instead of focusing on Kadan, I focused on *that,* letting my family take those endless pictures and *genuinely* smiling big as hell in each one. Once the pictures were done, I was whisked off to a surprise party that really was a surprise, where I ate, and danced, and drank, and laughed, and happy cried, and danced and ate and drank more, all to my heart's content.

It had been a long ass time since I felt so light.

I was still tipsy and happy and full in more than one way when I stepped off the elevator in my building. I'd thought long and hard about staying over with my sisters and cousins for a massive grownup sleepover, but all I really wanted to do was sleep in my own bed without an alarm the next day.

And check on *Miss Thing,* of course.

When I rounded the corner to my apartment, my steps slowed, taking in the sight of Kadan, sitting across from my door. He scrambled to his feet when he noticed me.

"What are you doing here?" I asked, convincing my legs to start moving again.

He smiled his smile – that goofy smile I adored – as he raked his fingers through his hair. "I was waiting on you at the 'doe... wow, that sounded so much less corny in my he—"

I didn't give him a chance to finish whatever the hell he was saying – I dove at him, crushing my mouth to his to start making up for the weeks of kissing we hadn't done. He immediately snaked his arms around my waist, hauling me into him to take over, which I didn't mind in the least.

I was just glad he was there.

Glad he was just as pressed as I was.

"You weren't at the ceremony," I blurted, as soon as we came up for air.

"Because I didn't want to make *your* day about me," he shot back, just as quickly. "But then I couldn't fuckin' stay away. I hit up Jason and asked him to let me know when you were on the way home."

I raised my eyebrows. "*I* didn't even know I was leaving until like ten minutes ago. And *you* live about ten minutes from here too."

"Oh, I never told you, did I? My middle name is Usain."

"Is *not*," I laughed. "But I guess this means you still like me?"

"Did you think I would stop?"

"Duh."

"*No*," he chuckled. "Now I said I would wait until you were finished with school – you've graduated. You're all glowing, and happy and shit, you're feeling good... don't break my heart, Ms. Love."

"Like you broke mine?"

His eyes went wide. "Don't tell me that... that fucked with me. A lot."

"Same here," I nodded. "But I'll admit, I *did* need time. More than I knew. But I came to a conclusion I need you to not freak out about, or give more weight than you should."

"Okay, hit me," he said, looking me right in the eyes, ready for whatever I had to say. More ready to hear it than I was to say it, even though I'd been sitting with it long enough.

I pushed out a sigh.

"I think I might... love you," I admitted. "Just a little though. Like, right at the beginning, you know? And I know it's stupid soon to say something like that, but it's just the truth. So if me being a weirdo and saying that isn't too much of a turnoff, then—"

"Stop it," he interrupted, scooping me into his arms again. "I had a little realization myself, when I was doing everything I could to respect your space these last few weeks."

"And what realization was th—oh. *Duh.*"

"Yeah," he laughed. "I think I might love you too."

the end.

ABOUT THE AUTHOR

Christina C. Jones is a modern romance novelist who has penned many love stories. She has earned a reputation as a storyteller who seamlessly weaves the complexities of modern life into captivating tales of black romance.

ALSO BY CHRISTINA C. JONES

The Lies – The Lies We Tell About Life, Love, and Everything in Between

Friends & Lovers:

Finding Forever

Chasing Commitment

Strictly Professional:

Strictly Professional

Unfinished Business

Serendipitous Love:

A Crazy Little Thing Called Love

Didn't Mean To Love You

Fall In Love Again

The Way Love Goes

Love You Forever

Something Like Love

Trouble:

The Trouble With Love

The Trouble With Us

The Right Kind Of Trouble

If You Can (Romantic Suspense):

Catch Me If You Can

Release Me If You Can

Save Me If You Can

Inevitable Love:

Inevitable Conclusions

Inevitable Seductions

Inevitable Addiction

The Wright Brothers:

Getting Schooled – *Jason & Reese*

Pulling Doubles – *Joseph & Devyn*

Bending The Rules – *Justin & Toni*

Connecticut Kings:

CK #1 *Love in the Red Zone* – *Love Belvin*

CK #2 *Love on the Highlight Reel*

CK #3 – *Determining Possession*

CK #4 – *End Zone Love* – *Love Belvin*

CK#5 – Love's Ineligible Receiver – Love Belvin

CK # 6 - *Pass Interference*

Printed in Great Britain
by Amazon